"*Secret Legacy kept me spellbound from page one to the very last word! The tension and relationships are beautifully written and will keep readers coming back for more. I got chills up my spine more than once. I can't wait to see what happens next.*"

— JJ KING, USAT BESTSELLING AUTHOR

"*A whimsical tale that will transport you from the first page.*"

— CARLYLE LABUSCHAGNE, USAT
BESTSELLING AUTHOR

"This book is packed full of awesomeness! Supernatural academy? Check. A girl who feels like she doesn't belong? Check. Sexy, mysterious boy? Check. And alllll the secrets, twists, and turns to keep you flipping pages. You don't want to miss this one!"

— LIZA STREET, USAT BESTSELLING
AUTHOR

Original Copyright © 2020 Carissa Andrews

Published in 2020 by Carissa Andrews

Cover Design © Carissa Andrews

All rights reserved.

ISBN-13: 978-1-953304-05-6

CURSED LEGACY

Book 4 of the Windhaven Witches

CARISSA ANDREWS

CHAPTER 1
A LOT LIKE CHRISTMAS

I f you had told me two years ago that I was a
necromancer with postmortem-medium tendencies,
I would have laughed in your face. First of all,
because I didn't know what any of that meant. Second of
all, because I didn't even believe in ghosts. Besides, I was
just an ordinary girl, saving money for college so I could
become a forensic scientist.

But I would have been wrong.

Now, if you had added that I was a necromancer who
would ultimately fall in love with an Angel of Death-in-
waiting, but we'd both be cursed by the Moirai, better
known as frickin' *Fates*, for that love, I would have told you
it was time for your meds because you'd clearly gone off
the deep end. I'm not that girl.

Only... *I am.*

I'm all of those things.

It's been two months since I found out my dad was
dead, even though I'd been interacting with him for over a
year and didn't even know he was a ghost. Yeah, color me

clueless. I guess the Windhaven Academy can scratch *intuitive* off the list of powers I have. If this curse catches up with us, I'll never finish my schooling... Never become what I was *meant to be*.

Then again, maybe that's all life is. The perpetual evolution of taking what life throws at you so you can become more of who you already are.

Either way, if the Moirai catch up to us, no amount of schooling will keep us safe. It will be game over. Should they get what they want, there will be one less Blackwood and Hoffman in the world. Our lines will die out with us and the Moirai can walk away, wiping their hands clean of our unfortunate existence

We may as well spend the last few moments of our lives trying to make things right.

And at the very least, neither of us will die alone.

I hope.

Ambient morning light streams into my bedroom window and I can no longer settle into sleep. Instead, I prop myself up on my right arm, watching Wade as he sleeps.

His dark eyelashes dance across his cheeks as he dreams, and I find myself smiling as I wonder what fills his dreams. I hope they're more peaceful than my own.

Sleep hasn't been an easy endeavor for the longest time. I'm almost afraid to linger too long there. Besides, if my days are numbered, I want to be awake for as much of them as humanly possible.

With my left hand, I trace the outside circle of the strange mark on Wade's chest signifying his expulsion from his family's angel lineage. For weeks it was an angry lesion and it was a painful reminder of how much being together has cost him. It was painful just to look at before, but as the skin has healed, the scar is almost beautiful, in its own way. The outer circle is delicate, with an air that's reminiscent of a ring of fire. Inside, three triangles all intersect.

Wade's head lolls to the side, his eyelashes fluttering from my touch.

"Mmmm," he sighs happily, a smile sliding across his features. "I could wake up to your touch every day."

"Are you sure it doesn't hurt?" I ask, meeting his gaze.

His silver eyes take in my every move, even through partially closed lids. He shakes his head, resting his hand on top of mine. "No, not anymore."

I frown, wishing there had been some way to spare him from the pain of any of it. Had I been able to keep my distance and just stayed away from him...maybe he'd be better off right now. Maybe none of this would have happened.

Then again, without Wade, who knows where I'd be. Or how I would have helped my dad. Maybe I'd still be fighting his Lemure—or worse. *Maybe I'd be dead.*

I shudder away the thought.

"Have you heard anything more from your mom?" Wade asks, tickling the space between my thumb and index finger.

I scrunch my face. "Not since the other day. I tried her last night, but she's taking things a lot harder than I thought she would."

"Even if your parents weren't together anymore, they still had a shared bond. They had you," Wade whispers.

"I know. But we never really talked about him," I

mutter, dropping back down on my side and resting my cheek against his chest.

He runs his left hand across my upper back, making my skin tingle. "Maybe it was hard for her to talk about him? They separated after what happened to you. There's gotta be a lot of mixed-up feelings in there."

"Yeah, I suppose," I say, nodding. "I'll try her again in a couple of hours. Let her get up and moving for the day before I call. It's Saturday and she likes to sleep in, if she can."

"Plus, she must be a little floored by the daily check-ins," Wade chuckles.

"True," I say, laughing under my breath.

It's not that I didn't want to connect more with her. It's just that... it's been hard. Moving out to Windhaven has consumed all of my time. The mysteries and life-or-death situations have captured my attention and held onto it with a viselike grip.

Luckily, she hasn't taken any of that to heart. She's just as independent as I am that way. I guess the apple doesn't fall far from the tree.

"What about the others?" Wade asks, laying his hand flat against my arm.

I sigh. "I talked to Cat last night. She said that Colton's back to his full strength, but even Diana was surprised at how long it took. But other than that, things are still going well with their training. Diana and Blake have been really good for them, I think."

"That's good. I mean, on all fronts."

I tip my chin upward, looking him in the eye. "Even the part about Colton? Are you getting soft in your old age, Mr. Hoffman?"

Wade chuckles. "I don't have time for grudges. Besides, the guy might have saved my life. Before he did"—his eyes narrow—"whatever he did that day...things were so foggy. Garbled, you know?"

"Yeah, I get it," I whisper, dropping my gaze.

For a while there, I had thought I'd lost Wade, and I don't overly want to relive those moments.

"It was probably just a concussion, but who knows? It coulda been way worse, too. So, I gotta have gratitude. You know?" Wade says.

I nod, chewing on the side of my lip.

"All right, enough moping. Come on," he says, twisting out of my embrace and sitting up on the bed. The blankets slide down around his waist, but he pulls his shirt on before I even get the chance to admire his form.

I groan, lying back down in bed. "But I was comfortable."

Wade laughs, chucking his pillow at me as he stands up. "Get up, Dru. We've got some things to do today."

"We do?" I say, peeking out from under the pillow.

A dazzling grin spreads across his gorgeous features, melting my resolve. "All right," I mutter, begrudgingly getting out of bed. I may have been the first one awake, but it doesn't mean I wanted to be up and moving around.

After a quick breakfast of Pop-Tarts and Red Bull, we're in Wade's car, traveling to goodness knows where. All I know is it's been over an hour, with no end in sight.

"Why won't you tell me where we're going?" I ask, quirking an eyebrow.

Wade's cheeks mound as he shakes his head. "Woman, you'll know soon enough. Just enjoy the drive, would you?"

I flit my gaze to the snow-covered landscape. We got

our first blanket of the white stuff two nights ago. Despite being only a couple of weeks away from Christmas, not even the more festive landscape has been able to lighten my mood. It hasn't even gotten me into the spirit of the holiday. By now, I'd be chomping at the bit to get up holiday decorations and listen to Christmas music.

But after everything that happened with my dad, I can't seem to find my joy.

Wade reaches over, taking my hand in his and bringing it to his mouth. He kisses the top of my hand and rests it, still interlocked with his, on the center console.

"If it makes you feel any better, we're nearly there," Wade says, shooting me a sideways glance.

I narrow my gaze.

"Don't give me that look, Ms. Blackwood. It doesn't suit your pretty face," he says, smirking.

"Hmph." I lean back in the seat, staring straight ahead. "Aren't we getting kinda close to Mistwood Point? We're not going to see Mom, are we?"

Wade laughs. "No, but now that you mention it, we could swing by later, if you want."

I scratch the side of my temple, trying to figure out where he's taking me. It's been so long since we went anywhere just for fun that the thought of decoding his actions literally makes my head hurt and my stomach uneasy.

Swallowing hard, I lean back in the seat and close my eyes.

When I open them again, Wade's pulling into a parking lot the size of the entire city of Windhaven.

"Did I fall asleep? Where are we?" I ask, rubbing my eyes.

"We have just landed at the CambridgeSide Mall," Wade says, his face lit with a mischievous glow.

I can't stop my eyebrows from rising into my hairline. "You brought me to Cambridge? To go to a mall?"

Wade scoffs. "It's not just a mall. It's a journey to *Christmasland*."

Snickering under my breath, I turn to face him. "Please tell me that's not a reference to turning into a vampire in the back of a Rolls Royce Wraith."

"Only if you want it to be," he says, chuckling. "No, this is meant to be a good, old-fashioned Christmas-y outing to get you interacting with the world again. Besides, I need to get some hints on what you want as a present." He shoots me a sly grin.

"Ah, so ulterior motives, then?"

"Always," he laughs. "Now are you coming with me, or what?"

Wade kicks his door open, letting in a bluster of cold winter air. I shudder, but unbuckle my seat belt and follow him.

The moment we get inside the massive glass structure, we're inundated by the sights and sounds of the holidays. Decorations of wreaths, trees, and fake snow adorn all of the walkways, and kiosk areas. Holiday music blares throughout the building, enticing even my dormant love for Christmas to come out and play.

"Where would you like to go first?" Wade asks, spinning around in the main entry. "The possibilities are endless... Macy's? Sephora? Best Buy? *Victoria's Secret?*" He grins broadly, wiggling his eyebrows suggestively.

I can't help but laugh. "You pick. I've never been to a mall this big."

"Never?" Wade asks incredulously.

I shake my head. "No, never. We mostly stuck around Mistwood Point. My mom's kind of a homebody."

"Well, my dear Dru, this is a bigger occasion than originally anticipated," Wade says, reaching out for my hand. As I respond, he wraps my hand around his forearm, and places his hand over top. Tipping his chin high, he declares, "We shall see them all."

We spend the entire rest of the day in the mall, taking the shops at our leisure and enjoying every minute of it. I don't remember the last time I spent any amount of time lately just relaxing and enjoying the day. In fact, it's probably been years. At least before moving here.

For a few blissful hours, even the craziness waiting for us when we return home escapes my mind. We looked at comics, new laptops in the Apple Store, movies in Best Buy, everything in the game store, and Wade even came with me into Kay Jewelers.

By the time we were spent—both physically and monetarily—it was edging near suppertime.

"They have a Cheesecake Factory? Oh, *yes please*," Wade says, sighing with delight. "You're going to love this one. Let me see if they have any openings." Without another word, he runs off, leaving me standing in the middle of the walkway with our haul.

"Okay, I'll just..." I say, spinning around and looking for the nearest bench, "wait right here." Luckily, it isn't far, but maneuvering through the crowd of shoppers is awkward with so many bags.

When I reach the bench, I detangle my hands from the bags and drop them on the seat. My fingers contort into odd angles, and anyone watching me would think I was mimicking a velociraptor as I tried to stretch them back out.

Suddenly, someone slams into me from behind. I stumble forward, trying to catch my balance on the bench and reaching for my purse as it tumbles off my shoulder.

"Sorry," the woman mumbles, continuing onward toward the exit in a hurry.

She tugs on a pair of gloves and as she pulls up the hood on her coat, something sparkly tumbles out of it, landing on the tiled floor.

"Hey, wait. You dropped something," I call out, rushing forward and bending down to pick it up off the floor.

Despite my calls, the woman continues onward, oblivious to the rest of the world. Sighing to myself, I shake my head and take a closer look at what she dropped. In the palm of my right hand is nothing glittery at all. In fact, what rests there is a tattered red thread. My head snaps up as I frantically try to find the woman again in the crowd.

But she's gone.

Every cell in my body hums in anticipation as fear grips me.

This was no accident.

This was the Moirai sending me a warning.

CHAPTER 2

THE ROLLER COASTER OF A
CURSED LIFE

My head spins and I take a seat on the bench. The entire mall could be on fire and I'd never even notice it. Instead, all I can think about is...

How much time do I have left?

"Well, it looks like there's about an hour—" Wade pulls up short as he sees the look on my face. "What is it? What's wrong?"

I hold out my hand, palm side up. No words necessary.

Wade plucks the red string from my hand, bringing it closer. The color drains from his face, like the string pulls it straight out of his skin.

"Where did you get this?" he whispers, crumpling the string and tossing it in the nearest garbage. Then, slowly, he takes a seat beside me.

"A woman dropped it," I whisper. Blinking back my daze, I point toward the main exit, as if he'd somehow be able to still see her.

Wade looks over the sea of people strolling in and out,

completely unaware that anything supernatural was happening in their midst.

"Is she still here?" he asks, turning back to me.

I shake my head. "No, she was gone before I even realized what she'd dropped."

"Why did you pick it up?" he asks. "Maybe it wasn't meant for you."

My mouth is suddenly devoid of all moisture, and I flick my tongue across my lower lip. "I didn't realize what it was. It looked shiny when it fell. I thought it was a piece of jewelry or something."

Wade's eyes again dart across the space. "We need to go. It's not safe here."

He stands up, grabbing hold of my arm and urging me to rise.

I do as I'm asked, barely able to wrap my head around picking up our bags, or making my feet move.

"We haven't even finished wrapping up my dad's affairs. The will... The house. Oh, my god. *Mom*," I mutter, wheeling through all of the worst-case scenarios.

Wade whirls around, grabbing my face in his hands. "Stop. Stop this—we are going to figure out what to do. I promise you. We're not going down without a fight."

"But you don't know—and my dad," I say, my words tumbling out in short sobs. "He tried."

"I know, I know," he murmurs, pulling me in close.

I lean into him, wishing his embrace could whisk me away. If he were an angel, like he was meant to be one day, he could just wrap me in his arms and fly away for all I care.

Without a word, Wade lets go of me. He spins around, grabbing hold of my hand and leading me through the exit.

The blustery winter wind whips at my hair, tossing it up like I'm on a roller coaster. And I guess in a way, I am.

The roller coaster that is a cursed life.

"I'm sorry, Autumn. I thought this day was going to take us away from all of this," Wade mutters as we get into his car. Shaking his head, he slams his hands against the steering wheel.

"It's not your fault," I say.

Wade snickers as he starts the car. Putting the car into drive, he spins out of the parking lot, racing away from the mall like it's on fire.

We drive in silence for nearly a half hour. Darkness has descended on us, but the headlights and array of Christmas lights cast a magickal aura across the landscape as we traverse it.

"I was going to take you ice skating," Wade whispers, tilting his head as he stares out at the road ahead of us.

"What?" I ask.

"There's a really beautiful outdoor ice-skating rink. It's got Christmas trees and twinkle lights... I wanted to take you to it," he says, shaking his head.

"Oh," I say. My eyelashes flutter as I process this information.

"I love you, Autumn. With everything that's happened, I don't want us to lose sight of that," he says, a hint of sadness lingering between his words.

"I'm not..." I start, but bite back my words.

I haven't lost sight of it... Have I?

"We deserve to be happy. Even just a little bit. You know?" Wade continues.

Tears well under my eyelids and I nod. "Yeah."

"We're not going to be safe until we put all of this

behind us. The Moirai will keep coming. They'll taint anything good until there's nothing left of us," he says, clenching his jaw. "I won't let that happen."

"I agree."

Wade sighs, pausing for a moment. "I won't be going back to Windhaven Academy in January. Now that I've been permanently expelled, I don't have the funds—or a magickal reason to be there."

My heart is suddenly very heavy, and I stare out of the passenger-side window.

It's all because of me.

"If you don't go, I won't either," I say, pressing my lips tight.

"Don't be ridiculous. That's not why I was telling you."

"Think about it, Wade. You said it yourself. The Moirai aren't going to stop. I can't just go back to school and act like I'm not being hunted. That *we're* not being hunted. We need to end this. Find a way to break the curse. I can't do that at Windhaven Academy," I say, snorting to myself. "I highly doubt they have a class on curse-breaking or circumventing fate."

Silence settles in the vehicle as he gives my words some thought. After a few minutes he finally says, "Maybe you're right."

"I know I'm right," I say, sitting up straighter and paying more attention to the scenery. "Are you taking us to Mistwood?"

"After what just happened, Windhaven's too far. I thought we could crash here for the night. Besides, it will give you some time to talk to your mom," Wade says, turning toward the city.

CARISSA ANDREWS

"She's not going to want to talk about it. I could barely get her to say two words on the phone."

"Then at least you can sit with her and be in her presence," Wade says. "Don't ever take that for granted."

Guilt coils in my stomach, and I know he's right. I wish like hell that I had spent more time with my dad when he was alive. Now, it's too late.

It takes less than ten minutes before we're pulling into my mom's driveway. Despite having grown up here, it feels strange now, showing up unannounced.

We don't even get the chance to open our car doors before Mom's outside, wrapping her sweater around her as she stands on the front porch.

"Hi, Mom," I say, walking up the stairs and wrapping my arms around her.

"Hey, sweetie," she says, pulling me in tight.

It's been a month since I last visited in person, and every time, I wonder why it takes so long to come back home. Her embraces are one of the only things on this planet that have the power to calm my nerves.

"Hi, Wade," Mom says, flicking her wrist and inviting him in on the action.

He steps forward, stretching his arms out wide to incorporate us both into his hug. For the longest moment, we just stand there, breathing in the cool air and clinging to each other.

"Come on, ladies. As much as I love you both, I don't want us to freeze to death out here," Wade says, chuckling softly and trying to keep things light.

Mom and I nod as he reaches around, opening the door for us.

Once we're inside, Mom casts me a sideways glance, nodding toward the kitchen. We follow her.

"What are the two of you doing here? Did I know you were supposed to be here?" Mom asks, her hazel eyes switching between the two of us.

Wade shakes his head. "No, we were in Cambridge and —" he stops, shooting me a glance that will instantly put my Mom's Spidey senses up.

As if on cue, she quirks an eyebrow and turns to me. "Autumn?"

I stare at her for a moment, trying to look casual. "It's nothing. We just thought we'd stop by and say hello."

She narrows her eyes, clearly not buying it.

I fiddle with the bottom of my coat, trying to avoid looking either of them in the eye.

"Autumn found a red thread today," Wade blurts out.

My head whips around to him. "Traitor," I say.

Wade's silver eyes are empathetic as he reaches for me. "After everything, she deserves to know."

Mom's eyes are wide as she glances between us. "Thank you, Wade. I'm glad Autumn has someone like you in her life. Since she clearly doesn't want to include me in it."

"Mom," I groan. "That's not it at all."

"No, no. I get it. I didn't want any of this for you. Right? So how could I possibly understand what's going on now?" she spits, her eyes flashing. "Is that it?"

"Of course not," I say, shaking my head. "I didn't want to worry you."

She actually snorts out loud. "That is the most ridiculous thing I've heard you say."

"Mom, I don't want to fight. Please," I say, dropping my shoulders in defeat. "This is hard enough without—"

"Ladies," Wade interjects, holding his arms out between us. "You need each other now, more than ever. Andrea, Autumn might not have been the one to say it, but I know she wanted to. She wants you in her life—her *real life*. Not just the superficial stuff. She wants to be able to lean on you with this shit. We have some heavy things coming at us and she just needs..."

"Her mom," she whispers. Blinking back tears, Mom sighs and walks over to me. "I'm sorry, sweetie. It's just... I wanted to keep you safe and the only way to do that was to keep you from all of this. I know its allure, trust me. But I can't help it. I still wish you'd never opened that damn packet."

"Mom, the Windhaven Academy had nothing to do with this. I am who I am. It's in my blood. Acceptance to the school only shone the light on it," I say, shrugging. "Ignoring it wouldn't have kept the Moirai from me. It would have only kept me in the dark."

"Wouldn't that have been better?" she asks, grabbing hold of my hands. Her eyes plead with me, begging me to understand.

Shaking my head, I drop my gaze to our hands. "No, it wouldn't."

"How can you say that?" she asks as tears slide down her cheeks. "This life—it killed your father and so many others. Now, it's trying to claim you, too."

"And dying in ignorance would be a waste," I whisper, fighting back my own tears. "I need to stop them, Mom."

"You can't stop them. Your dad *tried*," she sobs, clutching my hands tighter. "He spent his life trying to protect you."

"I know that now," I say, shooting my blurry gaze to Wade.

His chin tips upward as he tilts his head to the side and rubs my shoulder.

"But now it's my time to protect myself," I say, dropping her hands and wrapping my arms around her neck. "I just need your love and support."

"Sweet girl, you've always had that," she says, brushing her hand over the back of my head.

Closing my eyes, I lean into her body, wishing I could stay in that protective cocoon forever. But deep down, I know the world isn't so kind. Bad things are still coming for us.

The question is, *how soon?*

CHAPTER 3

PHONE CALLS & EXPLORATION

Being around Mom turned out to be just the thing I needed to feel more centered, but unfortunately, the feeling didn't last long. By the time we were on the way back to Windhaven, all the anxiety that was pressing on us before we left welcomed me back with open arms.

In fact, the pressure was almost worse. Before we left, things were at least calm. There were no signs, no strings...

But now?

Our education is on hiatus and we've officially been put on notice by the Moirai.

Terrific.

"I think we should check out more of the books in your dad's study. I was researching the other day and it turns out, he really had quite the collection of obscure texts. Maybe there's something useful in there on helping us stop the Moirai?" Wade says, pulling out a large knife to dice the onion in front of him.

I close the refrigerator and toss him the tomato in my hand. He catches it with ease and smirks.

"I guess I'm not overly surprised after reading my dad's journal. He was working hard to stop the Moirai. If anyone has the intel we need, it would have been him." I pause, my forehead creasing as I think about all the time lost. There is so much I should have asked him.

"Hey, hey..." he says, setting down the knife and walking over to me. "I know that look."

Before I think of anything else to say, his arms wrap around me. I set my cheek against his shoulder, leaning into him. Sandalwood and soap are the smells of home now, and I inhale them deeply, letting them wash away my worry.

Suddenly, the phone on the kitchen counter rings, echoing through the room like an alarm. We jump apart, but I shake off the surprise to walk over to the cordless.

I don't even look at the caller ID.

"Hello?"

"Is Mrs. Blackwood available?" a woman on the other end asks.

"This is Ms. Blackwood," I say, not feeling the need to correct her any more than that.

There's silence for a moment, then shuffling of some papers. I scrunch my face and shoot Wade a sideways glance.

"Who is it?" he mouths.

I shrug in response.

Finally, the woman clears her throat. "Ah, yes. Ms. Blackwood. Is your mother there?"

"No, my mother doesn't live here. What can I do for you?" I say, rolling my eyes.

"This is the law office of Harper, Lance, and Scott. We're finalizing the last will and testament of Lyle James Blackwood and wish to schedule a reading of the will next Monday," the woman on the other end declares.

"Oh, I see," I say, clearing my throat.

"We would like to come out to Blackwood Manor, if this works for your family. Should I call Mrs. Blackwood to make arrangements?" she asks.

I clutch the phone to my ear but swap it to the other side. "That won't be necessary. I'm the one who lives at Blackwood Manor."

"It's imperative Mrs. Andrea Blackwood be in attendance," the woman says.

"Okay, I'll see what I can do," I say, narrowing my gaze as I try to figure out why she's so adamant about my mother.

There's another pause. "Excellent. What time shall we put you down?"

"How about one p.m.? My mom lives in Mistwood Point, so it will take her some time to get here," I say.

"That'll do. We have you down. Someone from our firm will be out there at one p.m. on Monday, Ms. Blackwood. Have a nice evening."

The woman hangs up before I can say anything. I pull the phone back, staring at the keys.

"Who was that?" Wade asks, standing beside the diced vegetables with a look of concern.

I screw up my face, setting the phone back on the cradle. "It was the law firm handling my dad's estate. They want to do the reading of the will next Monday."

Wade takes a step toward me. "That's good, isn't it? I

mean, it's taken a while to prove his death and get things in order."

"Yeah, it's good, I guess," I nod. "At least, it will be when it's over."

Wade's eyebrows knit together. "What's wrong then?"

I pause, thinking back to the conversation. "She was really pushy about my mom. She wants me to make sure she's here."

"Why is that so weird?"

"Because they've been divorced for more than a decade?" I say, leaning against the counter. "I mean, is it normal to want your ex at the reading of your will?"

"Well, he did share something pretty important with her," Wade says, raising his eyebrows knowingly and pointing at me.

"Yeah, I know. I guess I didn't expect to have to bring her here. She's not going to like it," I say.

"Do you think he left something in the will for her?" Wade asks.

I shrug. "Probably? Why else would she be so pushy about it?"

Wade chuckles, taking the last few steps to me. He kisses my cheek and says, "Good point. We can call your mom in a little bit and let her know. It'll all be fine."

Exhaling slowly, I tip my head. I seriously hope he's right.

"I have to admit it's kinda weird, though. It's like the roles are totally reversed from when my grandpa died," Wade says, returning to his chopping.

"Yeah, it does have a weird déjà vu vibe, doesn't it?" I say, nodding and walking over to the pantry to grab spaghetti noodles. "Let's hope things don't go as sideways as they did after your grandpa died."

"On the upside, his bones are already interred in the catacombs. I think it's pretty safe to say you won't find him in the middle of the yard as a revenant," Wade says, stirring in the tomato sauce.

"Good point," I nod, handing him the package of noodles.

After dinner, we sit in relative silence. My brain keeps dragging me back to the will, the reading, and telling my mom that she needs to be here. I know if I don't get that call over with, my stomach will be in knots all night.

Wade studies me, his light eyes taking in my every move.

"What's got you frowning?" he finally asks.

Pressing my lips into a thin line, I shake my head. "I need to call my mom. I just don't know what to say."

"How about, 'Hi, mom. I got a call from the lawyer and they want to do the will reading next Monday. Any chance you can be there?'" he says nonchalantly.

"Easy for you to say. You didn't grow up with her," I mutter.

"Come on. She's not that bad," Wade says, chuckling. He stands up, reaching for my plate and placing it on top of his own. "Call her. I'll get the dishes done and then we can hang out. Trust me, it's not going to be as bad as you're making it out in your head."

"But I really should help," I say, moving to stand up.

Wade sets the dishes down and puts his hands on my shoulders before I can get up. "Stop trying to postpone the inevitable. I'm not that bad at doing dishes. Yeesh."

I fall back into my seat, and my gaze travels to my cell phone resting face down in the middle of the table.

"But..." I begin.

Wade leaves the room and yells, "Call her."

Blowing out a puff of air, I reach for the phone and flip it over. Staring at the screen, it takes me another couple of minutes to build up the courage to call her over this. Any other time, for any other thing, and it would be no problem. But this is a double whammy — dealing with death and under supernatural circumstances.

I press Mom's number before I have time to talk myself out of the call. The phone rings and as it cycles into the third ring, relief washes over me.

It's abruptly cut off as the ringing stops and Mom says, "Hey, sweetie. What a nice surprise. Everything okay?"

My eyebrows scrunch in and I pinch the bridge of my nose. "Hi, Mom. Uhm, yeah, everything's great."

"Uh-oh. I know that tone. What's up, young lady?" Mom says, obviously using her own superpowers, also known as motherhood, on me.

I clear my throat. "Well, I uh..." Taking a deep breath, I try to remember what Wade's version sounded like. "I got a call from the attorney handling Dad's stuff. He, uh... evidently, he needs you to be here for the will reading on Monday."

There's a long pause on the other end and I pull the phone back to see if we got disconnected. The timer is still continuing to log the duration of the call.

"Mom?"

"I can't make it," she finally says.

"Why?"

"I don't want anything to do with that place. I know—"

She sighs heavily. "I know it's your home now, and I suppose it should be now that... But I don't have the fondest of memories there."

"But Mom—"

"Enough, Autumn. I'm sure that if the attorneys want to get ahold of me, they'll find a way. Now, what about Christmas? Do you and Wade have plans yet?" she asks, adeptly changing the subject.

"No, not yet," I say, getting up and staring out into the darkness beyond the dining room window. The moonlight sparkles across the snow, lighting the landscape in its silvery glow.

"Well, how about the two of you come here for a few nights. We can spend Christmas Eve and day together."

"Okay, I'll see what Wade thinks," I say, nodding absently.

"Good. Let me know what you two decide, so I can put a plan together," Mom says. "Love you, Autumn."

"Love you, too, Mom."

"Talk to you later, sweetie."

"Okay, bye, Mom." I end the call, dropping the phone to my side.

I hope she's right about the lawyers because I'm pretty sure they don't want to just see me. Shaking my head, I turn and walk into the kitchen.

Wade is finishing up the dishes as I walk into the room, and he turns to face me. "See, nothing to it. On both accounts," he beams. "So, what did she say?"

I shake my head. "She said...*no*."

"No?" He quirks an eyebrow at me and scoffs as if I'm lying.

"Dead serious. She even changed the subject and asked about Christmas," I say, setting my phone on the counter.

"Gee, you weren't kidding. She really doesn't want to deal with this place."

I nod. "Ya think?"

"Okay, well, what's plan B? Are you going to call the lawyer back?" Wade asks, wiping his hands on a dish towel.

"No, I'll just let it ride. If they turn up here and my mom's not, then I'll proclaim innocence. She seems to think that if they want to get ahold of her, they'll find a way."

"There's probably truth in that," Wade says, tipping his chin.

"Well, either way...at least the call is over. What do you want to do now?" I ask, biting the inside of my cheek.

"Feel like doing some exploring? We still have a ton of rooms in the house we haven't checked out yet," he suggests, setting the cloth on the counter.

I shrug. "Sure. I don't think I could sit still, anyway. Too much nervous energy."

"Perfect," he says, jutting out his arm. "Our exploration awaits."

Laughing, I loop my arm through his and follow his lead.

The past few months have been a blur of epic proportions. I barely remember my own name, let alone all of the events that have happened since I found out my dad was dead and haunting the manor as a Lemure.

I vaguely remember asking Wade to move in with me so I didn't have to be alone. To this day, I still don't know if he's technically all in, or if his apartment is still his.

All I know is, he's here and it's where I want him to be. We're safer together.

"What about that corridor?" Wade asks, pointing to the wing that goes past the kitchen and heads toward the pond.

"Sure," I say, shrugging. In all honesty, it makes no difference to me. They're almost all the same, anyway. Strange bedroom-like rooms with old furniture from times gone by. Most of it smells like mothballs and dust.

The exceptions, of course, are the rooms like the art room upstairs I discovered last year or the study.

"What is it you hope to find?" I ask as we start walking down the dim corridor. The old electric sconces are lit, but the wattage on the bulbs is so low you practically need a flashlight to walk down them anyway.

Wade shrugs. "Nothing, really. It just gives us something to do other than sit in the bedroom or on the couch."

"True," I say, nodding.

The house is beautiful, and seeing some of the other rooms has opened my perceptions to its true size. It's almost like a map that's colored itself in further, inviting you into places you never knew existed.

The first few rooms are pretty standard. Dark, gothic wallpaper with gold embellishments. Plenty of furniture draped with white sheets.

"Your family sure did like having lots of rooms. Do you think they were ever all in use?" Wade asks as we close the fifth door behind us.

I shrug. "I'm not sure. I never really..."

Wade squeezes my hand. He already knows why.

"Well, I think it's pretty amazing. And to think... all of

this is going to be yours. No worrying about housing or money, really. It must be a relief," he whispers.

I blink back my surprise and stop walking. "You know, I never even thought about that."

"Really?" he says, raising an eyebrow.

"Yeah. I guess I've been so consumed by everything that I haven't given much thought to the house or whatever..."

"Not even when the lawyer called?" he chuckles. "Wow, trauma brain really has hit you hard."

"I guess it has."

"This whole house, the history that comes with it. Plus, you have your own family ghost..." he says, nudging me with his shoulder. "I wish I had something left of my family. Something...*enduring*."

I turn to him, my eyebrows tipping up in the middle. "Oh, Wade. I'm sorry."

He brushes his hand in the air. "Hey, no... It's no big. It's the way it's been my whole life."

"No, it's not. You always had one thing to carry with you," I say, reaching out and touching the spot on his chest where the mark now resides.

He presses his palm to my hand, pulling me in close. "Yeah, well. Now I start a new family tradition. I can be the one who leaves a new legacy for them."

A smile spreads across my lips, but it quickly dies back. "If we live long enough to start new legacies. If the Fates..."

Wade presses a fingertip to my lips, cutting off my words. He shakes his head. "Thou shall not speak of them in this holy place," he says, mimicking Abigail's accent.

"Yeah, well, speak or not...they'll find their way in.

We're not clear of them. Especially after the mall," I say, reaching out to turn the handle of another door midway down the hall.

"I know. But until we have a concrete plan, we can't let that hang over our heads. We'll kill ourselves with worry," he says.

As I fling the door back, I pull up short at the surprisingly sparse setting. The decor on the walls is mostly the same—wallpaper and gold embellishments. But it's the single white cloth draped over a piece of furniture that pulls me up short.

"What do you think it is?" Wade asks, eyeing me mischievously.

"I have no idea," I mutter, trying to make sense out of the shape.

"Then let's take guesses. Hmmm..." he says, scratching at his chin. "I think it's an old workout room—that's why there's nothing else in here."

"Okay, so what's your guess," I chuckle.

"A bit obvious, really. It's an old-fashioned stationary bike," he declares.

I stare at it, surprised by how accurate a possibility his guess is.

"How am I going to compete with that?" I say, thrusting my arm out and pointing my upturned palm at the item.

"Just make a guess," he laughs.

I lower my eyebrows and cast him a sideways look. Stepping farther in the room, I edge a little to the left to get a different vantage point.

"I think you were close, but no cigar. It's clearly one of

those old circus bikes with one wheel that's bigger and one that's smaller," I say, holding my chin up high.

Wade shakes his head, chuckling under his breath as he walks forward. "All right... and the winner is..." In one fell swoop, he lifts the sheet. Dust flies into the air in a great plume, and we both take a step back, coughing.

There, underneath the sheet, is an old-fashioned spindle.

"Well, there you have it, ladies and gentlemen. My girl-friend is actually...*Sleeping Beauty*," Wade says, laughing as he turns to me.

But for me, it's no laughing matter at all. I remember what we learned about the Moirai.

Is this another one of their warnings?

CHAPTER 4
POMP AND CIRCUMSTANCE

Anxiety wells up inside me, making my stomach roll and churn. Before I know it, my spaghetti is on its way back up. I rush down the hall to the nearest bathroom, barely getting enough time to close and lock the door behind me before I empty the contents of my stomach into the toilet.

"Autumn? Autumn, are you okay?" Wade asks, pounding on the door. The handle jangles as he tries it but holds steady.

"Yeah, I'm fine. I'll be just a minute," I sputter.

Jitters consume my body and for a moment, it's all I can do to not pass out—or fall over. When they subside, I wipe the side of my mouth and lean back, resting my head on the wall behind me.

I shouldn't let things get to me like this. It isn't healthy. At this rate, I won't need the Moirai to finish me off. I'll end up doing it to myself.

"Seriously, Autumn. Are you okay?" Wade says, from the other side of the door.

Inhaling slowly, I push myself forward, crawling on all fours to the door. I pull myself up on the counter and unlock the door. Stepping back, Wade pushes it open.

"Sorry, I'm just a bundle of nerves. I saw that...spindle and it freaked me out," I whisper.

Wade's dark eyebrows furrow and he eyes me closely. "You look like death." He screws up his face. "Sorry. Kinda slipped out."

"I *feel* like death," I mutter. "It'll pass. I'm just too... *raw*."

Wade wraps his arms around me, pulling me into his chest. The heat from his body sends chills rolling through me as he attempts to warm me up.

"Come on. That's enough exploring for one day. Let's get you in bed," he says, leading us out of the bathroom and into the darkness of the hall.

The next few days pass in a blur of anxiety-induced bedrest. My stomach has continued to be persistently queasy, and anything I attempt to eat doesn't linger long inside my system. Between the family curse and the reading of the will, there's no safe place to settle into. I don't know how to relax anymore.

Before I know it, it's Monday.

The executor of the will will be arriving any minute, and I have yet to get dressed for the day.

"I don't wanna do it," I whine, lying back on the bed.

Wade laughs, reaching for my hand. "I know, but you need to get out of this bed anyway."

"Do I really, though?" I ask, lifting an eyebrow.

"Yes, you do. As much as I love you, you need a shower and fresh clothes."

"What are you saying? I stink?" I sit up, scoffing in mock offense.

"It's quickly getting there," he laughs. "Now, move it. You'll feel better afterward and then we'll get this reading over with. You'll feel better after all that, too."

I grumble, but shuffle my way to the bathroom. If the past couple of days in Wade's care wasn't enough to remind me of his time as a personal care assistant, it's evident as I walk into the room. Fresh clothing is laid out across the radiator, along with a towel. My brush and my usual cosmetics and girly products are strewn across the counter.

Smiling to myself, I turn the shower on and cast a glance into the hallway. I can barely make out my bedroom doorway from here, but it appears Wade has vacated the room for less-confined pastures.

I can't say I blame him. He's spent the past few days by my side.

As I remove my clothing and drop it into the hamper, I stop by the mirror, gaping at myself. Dark circles accentuate my hazel eyes and I look like I could compete in a goth makeup competition.

Making a face, I turn back to the shower and hurry to get in.

While the water feels good, it does nothing to quell the panic brewing inside of me.

Nothing ever prepares you for losing a parent. As much as I think I've gotten over it, one more thing crops up, bringing it all back. One day it's a picture in the hall. Another day it's a casual conversation. Then it's something more serious, like dealing with the will.

By the time I step out of the shower, the room is frigid in comparison.

Hurrying over to the radiator, I grab my towel, grateful that Wade thought to put it on top of the toasty heat. After I dry off and dress, I have to admit, I do feel better. Not quite like a full-fledged human being, but close enough.

I make my way over to the bedroom, just to make sure Wade's not there, unsurprised when he's not. Padding my way down the hallway, I'm surprised to hear voices as I close in on the grand staircase.

"Will Ms. Blackwood be attending?" a soft male voice asks.

"Yes, she was just getting ready. She'll be here momentarily," Wade responds, ever the gentleman. "Is there anything I can get for you while you wait? Coffee, tea?

"Water would be lovely. Thank you, Mr. Hoffman."

"Not a problem." Wade walks out of the sitting room just as I round the corner to the main entry. He walks over to me and places his hands on my upper arms. Kissing me on the forehead, he says, "Breathe. It'll all be over soon."

I inhale slowly through my nose. "So, he's in there?"

Wade nods. "But he won't bite. Just go in and introduce yourself. I'm getting him some water. Do you want anything?"

"Vodka?" I mutter.

"Probably not a wise choice, considering. How about some tea? I think I saw chamomile in there somewhere," he says, jabbing a thumb toward the kitchen.

I nod in response, turning to face the sitting room. "Okay, here goes nothing."

Wade drops his hands, squeezing one of mine as he continues on his way.

Straightening my shoulders, I walk down the remainder of the hallway and into the sitting room.

A rather thin man in a dark-blue suit stands up from the couch. He's no taller than I am as he walks up to me with his arm outstretched. I reach for it, shaking his hand. His light eyes are the color of amber, which are reflected in the undertones of his blond hair.

"Ah, you must be Ms. Blackwood," the man says. "Henry Peterson. I'm with Harper, Lance, and Scott."

"Hi, Mr. Peterson. Yes, I'm Autumn. It's nice to meet you," I say, taking a seat on the couch opposite him.

On the coffee table between us is a small stack of paperwork and a small wooden box.

Mr. Peterson also takes a seat, resting his hands on his knees. "Will *Mrs.* Blackwood also be joining us?"

I scratch my temple, trying hard not to make a face. "She really wanted to be here, but she wasn't able to get away from work."

Mr. Peterson's face darkens. "I see."

An awkward silence stretches between us and I lean forward, clearing my throat.

"She was pretty adamant that if anything pertained to her, you'd be able to find out where to reach her," I say, trying to gloss over the transgression.

His face tightens as his gaze drops to the stack of paperwork. "There is, indeed, much in here that pertains to her. However, we shall start with what your father has willed over to you, if that's all right."

I inhale sharply, nodding. "Sure."

"Okay, I have a water for you, Mr. Peterson. A

chamomile tea for you, Dru," Wade says, handing us both our drinks.

Mr. Peterson opens his mouth, appearing at first to offer his gratitude, but pulls up short. "Did you say, *Dru?*" His jaw hardens as he looks between us with a sense of suspicion.

Wade, on the other hand, laughs it off. "It's just a pet name for Autumn."

The startled gaze doesn't diminish on Mr. Peterson's face. "Before we get started, I think it might be best to see some form of ID."

"What? Really? She looks like the female version of her dad—" Wade sputters.

I reach out, placing a hand on Wade's forearm. I try to quell his annoyance with a significant glance. "Would you mind running to the bedroom and grabbing my purse?"

He sets down a third mug, presumably his own, on the coffee table. "Sure."

Without another word, Wade walks out, shaking his head and mumbling under his breath. I'm pretty sure I heard the word *ridiculous* in the middle of the tirade.

"Sorry about that. We'll take care of any confusion," I say, sitting up straighter.

"Indeed," Mr. Peterson says, pursing his lips.

Rather than speak, the two of us sit in ghastly, uncomfortable silence, listening to the sound of the large clock on the wall tick the seconds away.

"And just who is this?" Abigail says, appearing to my right.

I let out a squeal of surprise, and try to stifle it with my fingertips.

"Are you all right, dear?" Mr. Peterson says, looking around the room with wide eyes.

I pat at my chest and nod. "Sorry, yes. I just thought I..." I shake my head, realizing I have absolutely no alibi for something as odd as that.

"Yes?" he presses, leaning in.

"I thought I saw an animal run past the window just now," I say. It's not a great lie, but it's enough to make Mr. Peterson turn around and look out the window behind him.

I shoot Abigail a look of consternation. She shrugs, wandering over to the fireplace and lingering beside it.

"Well, I don't see anything now," he says, turning back around to face me.

"Here you go, my lady," Wade says, his voice somewhat deadpan as he hands the purse over.

I chuckle under my breath at his attitude. As much as he loves to be of service to others, he likes to do it on his own terms.

"Thanks, Wade," I say, reaching inside and digging out my driver's license.

When I find it, I pass it over to the executor, who eyes it more closely than someone who thinks I shouldn't be buying beer. After a moment, he passes it back to me, satisfied I am who I say I am.

"Well, let's get started, shall we?" he mutters, picking up the papers and placing them in his lap.

Wade takes a seat on the couch beside me, eyeing Mr. Peterson with as much suspicion as he was just doling out to us.

"Oh, the manly energy fills the air. It appears things

have not changed all that much in the face of men," Abigail chuckles.

I smile, dropping my gaze to my lap.

"So, to start with, I would like to extend my deepest condolences, Ms. Blackwood, for the tragic loss of your father," Mr. Peterson says in what I can only imagine is his ordinary pomp-and-circumstance tone.

"Thank you," I mutter, biting down on the side of my lip.

"I have the final will and testament, produced and notarized by your father. It was graciously handled not terribly long ago, so I feel very confident in its findings," he continues, passing me a copy of the will. "Now, rather than bore you with the details, I'll just skip ahead to the parts that pertain to you, if that's quite all right?"

I look over my shoulder at Wade, who just shrugs. My guess is he's just as happy to have this uncomfortable exchange done and over with as I am.

"Okay, that sounds fair," I say, turning back to him and nodding.

"Excellent. You will, of course, have all of the details in the documents there, should you want to know about any other aspects," he says, dropping the paperwork and picking up the small wooden box. With a twitch of his lips, he stands up and passes it over to me.

Confused, I take the box from him. The outer shell is decorated in elaborate carvings. However, there are no hinges, no locks. In fact, nothing to indicate it opens. Just a...*box*.

"What is this?" I ask, lifting my gaze to Mr. Peterson.

"I wish I knew," Mr. Peterson says. "I must say, it's had

the rest of us at the law firm very curious when I retrieved it from the safe deposit box for you."

I rotate it in my hands, looking for something, anything, that stands out on it that might explain why my dad would leave me something like this. Is it a key to fighting the Moirai? Or is it just an old family heirloom?

Discreetly, I look over my shoulder, trying to see if Abigail is still there. Sensing my question, she walks closer and bends down right beside me.

"I have never seen such a thing before," she whispers, eyeing it with the same bewilderment.

I shake my head. "I'm not sure what it is, either," I say, flipping it over.

"These look like they could be words," Wade says, pointing to some of the carvings along the corners.

"Well, I do hope you'll share with us the mystery of the box," Mr. Peterson says with a wistful longing in his eyes. It's clear the mystery of the box is the most excitement this guy has seen in years.

Tipping my head, I say, "I will do that."

"Now, other than the box," Mr. Peterson says, holding onto his lapel like he's about to give a great speech, "you have also been willed quite a nice lump sum."

Wade and I exchange a significant glance as Mr. Peterson takes a sip of his tea.

"How much?" I ask.

"Fifty-million dollars."

Wade spits out his tea. Then he wipes frantically at his knees.

"I'm sorry, did you just say fifty *million?*" he asks, blinking wildly.

My jaw hangs open and I don't quite have the words.

"Now, of course, the rest belongs to another beneficiary," Mr. Peterson says, almost as if he's somber about relaying that information.

"Wait—what about the house?" I say, suddenly alarmed.

"Well, I'm afraid the house doesn't belong to you," Mr. Peterson says.

"What?" I sputter. "You have to be kidding. Who else would my father will it to?"

Mr. Peterson sits up a bit straighter, tugging at his collar. "Well, to his *wife*, of course."

CHAPTER 5
PUZZLING

All thoughts in my brain tangle with one another as I grapple to make sense of what the executors said. The word *wife* being associated with *my dad* has completely short-circuited my inner dialogue.

Wade turns to me, clearly as baffled as I am. Shrugging, I return my gaze to Mr. Peterson.

"I'm sorry, you must be confused," I say, shaking my head. "My dad wasn't married. Are you sure you have the most up-to-date will?"

Mr. Peterson's light eyebrows tug in slightly, but his gaze flits to the paperwork. "No, I'm quite certain. As I said before, the will was notarized only a couple of weeks prior to Mr. Blackwood's presumed death."

"But that makes no sense," I say, wracking my brain for an answer. He'd never mentioned another woman being in the picture and I would have thought she'd be prowling the house if she had some sort of claim on it.

"I really don't wish to get into the middle of a family squabble. But this *is* why we requested Mrs. Blackwood be in attendance. There are some important estate docu-ments that require her signature," Mr. Peterson says, shuf-fling the paperwork in his lap. Then he reaches down, pulling up a briefcase stored by his feet. With a sideways glance at us, he files the extra papers inside and clicks the lock shut. "But I suppose you're quite right about reaching out to her. Our office will make arrangements to have this matter squared away."

I nod absently, realizing the craziness of his claim.

My mom and dad can't still be married... *can they?*

Does she even know? Or is this why she didn't want to be here? Because she knew I'd have questions that she didn't want to answer?

"Well, despite the unfortunate circumstances, I hope it lightens your heart to know your father loved you very much, Ms. Blackwood," Mr. Peterson says, standing up. "That's a very sizable inheritance. If you need any recom-mendations on financial planners, I would be happy to offer a few suggestions. Of course, nothing needs to be decided now."

"Thank you," I say, standing up as well. I set the small box down on the coffee table and extend my hand to him. "I appreciate you coming out here. It's been very informative."

Wade also stands, but remains quiet and reserved beside me.

"If you have any questions on the remainder of the will, please do give me a call. Here's my card, should you need it," Mr. Peterson says, handing me a small rectangular card. It's a thick, white piece of paper with gold letters embossed into the top that read *Harper, Lance, and Scott.*

"Thank you, I'll keep that in mind," I say, nodding as I

set it on the table beside the wooden box.

"And do let me know if you figure out that box," he says, grinning and tipping his chin toward it.

A halfhearted smile is as much as I can manage.

Wade must have sensed my agitation. He's the first to move, walking out of the sitting room and over to the front door to open it. Mr. Peterson and I follow him. For the briefest of moments, the executor turns to me as if he's going to ask another question or say something else, but instead fashions a smile and simply nods. Patting my shoulder, he walks out without another word, making his way down the front steps and over to his silver BMW parked in the front loop. With a quick nod, he settles into the vehicle and drives off.

The two of us stand there in relative silence, watching the car fade into the distance of the long driveway. When we can no longer make out the taillights, Wade closes the door.

"Well, that was..." he begins.

"Messed up?" I say, scratching at my eyebrow before walking back to the sitting room.

"I was gonna go with enlightening, but sure—that, too," he says, following me.

I return to my seat, staring at the coffee table as if it might come up and bite me at a moment's notice.

Wade sits down beside me, placing a hand on my leg. "Are you okay?"

"Of course she's not all right, foolish man," Abigail says, pacing in front of the fireplace.

I smile slightly, knowing Wade can't hear her admonishment.

Rubbing my hand across my forehead, I can't seem to

remove my eyes from the stack of paperwork. "I honestly don't know. I'm really confused."

"I can imagine," Wade says. "That was quite the bombshell there."

"You are not wrong," I mutter.

"On the upside, it's your mom who will have possession of the house. It's not like it's going to the state or some strange woman you've never met or anything. So unless she wants to sell the manor, chances are she's not going to be kicking us out anytime soon," Wade says, grinning sheepishly.

I blink back surprise. "I didn't even think of that."

"It was a lot to digest. But seeing as I just let my lease on the apartment lapse, I have to admit, I had a mini heart attack there for a sec," Wade says, scrunching the left side of his face. "But at least you'd be safe. You could buy a hundred houses, if that's what you wanted."

The thought of being forced out hadn't occurred to me, but it should have. Sure, we could find someplace new. However, with all that we're facing, the last thing I would want to do is add moving into the mix.

I glance up at Abigail. The look of concern on her face makes my heart thump awkwardly in my chest. When my mom finds out she owns the manor, she wouldn't sell it, would she? I mean, she knows Wade and I live here and had no intention of moving.

Then again, in her mind, it could be a possible way to get me back to Mistwood Point. She's definitely got no love lost for this place.

My forehead furrows and my stomach is queasy all over again. I swallow hard, trying not to let the anxiety make me sick.

"So, what do you think is up with the box?" Wade asks, picking it up and turning it over in his hands. He eyes it from every angle, taking in the writing and carvings with a careful eye.

"I don't know," I say, turning again to Abigail.

"That box is a conundrum. It wreaks of power, though of what kind, I know not," she says.

Wade shifts in his seat, setting the box back down. "Is Abigail here?"

I nod. "She doesn't know anything, though."

Wade's face darkens as he stares at the decorative embellishments. "Hmmm. It reminds me of something, but I can't put my finger on what."

"I've never seen anything like it before," I mutter.

"Well, your dad wouldn't have given it to you if it wasn't important. Did he mention anything about a box before..." Wade cuts his words off, eyeing me like I'm a bomb about to explode.

I scrunch my face. "No. I wish he did, though."

"I guess it's up to us to figure out the mystery of it, then," he says, placing a hand on my knee.

"Yeah."

"I would take extreme caution with that box if I were you," Abigail says, rubbing at the back of her hand. "However, the young man is quite right. There is more to that box than simply pretty carvings."

We sit in silence for a few minutes, each of us lost in our own tangled thoughts.

"I can't believe my mom would lie to me," I say, breaking the stillness.

Wade looks up, turning to face me with weary eyes. "Did she ever tell you outright that they were divorced?"

I search my memories, and for the life of me, I can't think of a single instance. She always said stuff like, 'since they separated,' or 'when your dad and I were together.' But I can't think of a definitive time when she said they'd divorced. It was just sorta *implied*.

I shake my head. "Now that you mention it, I don't know, actually. Everything is all muddled. It's like I can't even trust my own memories. Besides, there's that whole section of my past, particularly when they broke up, that's still blacked out from when I drowned."

Wade's eyebrows tug in. "Weird."

"Your mother has many secrets I suspect you know not of," Abigail says, locking eyes with me, then casting her gaze to the floor. "This is but one of a long line."

I bolt upright out of the couch. "What do you mean?"

"What's going on?" Wade asks, suddenly at my side.

I hold up a hand to have him wait.

Abigail straightens her stance and her lips press tight. "It is best she be the one to untangle her deceit."

"What kind of answer is that?" I sputter.

"What's she saying?" Wade whispers in my ear.

I turn to him, my heart beating wildly. "She's saying my mom's been lying about a lot, but she won't tell me what she means."

Casting my gaze back to Abigail, she's now vanished. Clearly not wanting to be grilled for more information.

Sighing, I walk to the window.

There are so many unanswered questions and the stakes are already high.

"What are you thinking about?" Wade asks, wrapping his arms around me.

"So many things," I say, staring into the snow-covered

trees.

"We'll get this all figured out. Remember, just take it a day at a time. That's really the best you can do," he says.

"I don't know what I was expecting from today"—my eyes widen as I turn to face him—"but this definitely wasn't it."

"What? You didn't expect to become a multi-millionaire?" he chuckles, brushing my cheek with the back of his hand.

I shrink back. "Ugh, I haven't even processed that bit of info yet."

"Yeah, you know things are messed up when that's the bit of news that falls most to the wayside," he says, rubbing the back of his neck.

"Right?" I nod.

"So, what do you want to do? Call your mom? Demand some answers?" Wade asks, his silver eyes taking in every movement I make.

"No, there's no point in calling. Even if I did ask her, there's no telling what she'll say. She might keep trying to lie." I bite down on my lip, a plan formulating in my mind. "Without being able to see her facial expressions or body language, I'd have to take her at face value."

"All right. So, what then? Wait until the lawyers catch up with her?" Wade asks.

I snicker. "Oh, hell, no. Get packed up," I say, pressing my lips tight. "We're going to spend Christmas in Mistwood Point."

My mother might be a lot of things, but I hope lying to a point-blank question isn't one of them. I need answers— answers only she can give me. If she kept her ongoing marriage a secret, what else is she hiding?

CHAPTER 6
FOR YOUR SINS

Christmas in Mistwood Point is likely to be an interesting one, at the very least. Despite my original hesitation, I'm absolutely certain I need to talk to Mom about all of this face to face. I doubt she'll see my questions coming, but at this point, who knows?

Plus, now might be a good time to give her the note I found in Dad's journal and ask her what she knows about the Moirai. And anything else, for that matter.

Abigail's insistence that my mom has more secrets has put me on edge and the last thing I want is to be caught off guard or put into a dangerous position because of my ignorance. I've dealt with enough of that and I'm so over it.

Shifting my thoughts from what's to come, I focus on the notepad in front of me. I haven't seen much of James since everything went down with my dad. But I'd hate for him to worry when we're not here. He's been like a grandpa almost, always checking in and making sure things are okay. Even now he refuses to talk to me about changing the arrangements until things are finalized with the estate. Who knows how long that will be?

"Okay, bags are in the trunk. Are you sure you don't want anything else? Snacks? Pillows?" Wade asks as he enters the kitchen.

Looking up from the note, I stop and think. "Yeah, maybe pillows would be smart."

With a tip of his head, Wade spins around, walking back the way he came. "On it," he calls out.

Smiling softly, I return my thoughts to the note, scribbling down the details of our trip so James knows he doesn't have to worry about us for a week or so. As I finish the note, I stare at the pad, remembering all the times my dad had found a way to communicate with James, even though he was dead. This notepad, for better or worse, was one item on this earthly plane that he had access to, and used frequently, to make it seem like he was alive. He definitely fooled me—and obviously fooled James, too.

Sighing to myself, I set the pen down and follow Wade. My stomach is tied in knots as I anticipate what my mom might say—or what she might try to avoid talking about. Regardless, all I know is there is too much at stake now to be vague, and I'm done being the one constantly left in the dark.

By the time I make it to the grand staircase, Wade walks out of the hallway, heading toward me with pillows in hand.

He smiles brightly—the kind that lights his face, evaporating any of the worry he's lingering onto—and it makes me pull up short and catch my breath. Sometimes I forget how handsome he is. Things have been so heavy...so dark.

"Thanks for grabbing those," I say, reaching for his hand. "I'm all done."

"Then let's hit the road, beautiful," he says, sliding his free hand in mind.

As I lock up the house, Wade makes his way to Blue and places the pillows in the back seat.

"Would you like me to drive?" he asks as the door slams shut.

I finish locking the door and twist around to him. "No, it might be a nice distraction to drive, actually."

Winking at me, he opens the passenger door and takes a seat. I follow him, shaking my head in amazement. He can still pull off winking and make it look so natural.

Slipping into the driver's side, I turn on Blue and shift into gear.

The drive to Mistwood Point is surprisingly pleasant. Despite the cooler temperatures, the sun shines brightly, casting its warm glow across the snow. It makes the powder sparkle across the landscape—the ground, the trees. Even the naked branches sparkle, as if the snow has somehow managed to cling to its surface. The roads, on the other hand, are clear and free of ice, making it a mindless trip in terms of driving.

Yet, somehow, despite this, I can't shake the sense of foreboding looming over me the closer we get. It's as though a cloud of oppression is edging in and the closer to my old hometown, the heavier it feels.

"You look a little better today. How has your anxiety been?" Wade asks, breaking the silence for the first time in twenty minutes.

I clutch the steering wheel, thinking it over. "Okay, I

guess. It comes and goes, depending on how much I over-think, I guess."

"Doesn't seem like it's as bad as it was," he says, shifting in his seat to place his silver gaze on me.

I shake my head. "No, not as bad."

"Good. I was beginning to worry," he says squinting at me as he rubs his temple.

"What about you?" I ask, narrowing my gaze between glances at the road.

His eyes widen. "What about me?"

"Are *you* okay?"

"Why wouldn't I be?" he asks, dropping his hand to his lap.

I scrunch my face and quirk an eyebrow. "Do you have a headache?"

"A little. I should have brought my sunglasses. It's bright out here," Wade says, leaning back in his seat and reaching for my hand. "I forget sometimes just how bright the snow can be when it's sunny."

"We could stop and get you a pair in the next town. I don't think we're far from Winchester," I say, squeezing his hand.

"Nah, it'll be okay," he says, his eyes drifting shut. "We're nearly there. I'll just close my eyes for a bit. That'll help."

"Okay, but if you change your mind, let me know."

"Of course," he says, grinning with his eyes still closed.

My lips press tight and I return my gaze out across the landscape. I'd hoped to have more company to help me keep my mind off of everything. Conversation helps keep the anxiety at bay, but then again, I haven't been a terribly good conversationalist so far anyway.

The remainder of the drive passes in relative silence. Wade drifts off into an easy sleep, while I'm left alone with my thoughts. As expected, anxiety rips through my ribcage and more than once, I have to remind myself to breathe so I won't be sick.

By the time we pull into Mom's driveway, the sky has turned a brilliant shade of pink as the sun is close to setting. The house is dark inside, and I suddenly regret not calling to warn Mom about our arrival today.

"Wade, we're here," I say, nudging him gently.

He rouses, sitting up straighter in his seat as he looks around sleepily. "Sorry about that. Did I doze off?"

I nod, laughing softly. "Like, for most of the trip."

He makes a face, wiping at his eyes. "At least the headache seems a bit better now."

"Good." I run my hand along his arm. "Well, at least you'll be well-rested to help me interrogate my mom." My stomach coils again into knots, writhing like a serpent unable to be tamed.

"Speaking of that, you ready for this?" he asks, still blinking back his grogginess.

I stare at the dark house for a moment before shaking my head. "Not in the least." With that, I take a deep breath and open my car door.

Wade follows me, trudging through the snow a couple of steps behind.

When I reach the door, I stand there, staring at it as if it's suddenly some massive obstacle between me and my future.

"Contemplating how the door will bring about world peace?" Wade asks, chuckling under his breath beside me.

I shoot him a sideways glance and lift my arm.

Knocking on the door a few times, I take a step back and wait. Mom will be thrilled to see us—that part is certain. It's what comes afterward that I'm worried about.

The two of us stand there a moment, listening for sounds of movement from inside, but everything remains dark. After another minute, I knock again.

"It's pretty dark in there. Do you think she's still at work?" Wade offers, looking at his watch.

"Maybe?" I say. Truthfully, I've been so far out of the loop now, I don't know what her normal routine looks like anymore.

I reach for my phone, pulling it from my coat pocket. Punching the keys for her number, I turn and face Wade, swapping my stance from foot to foot to warm up. The phone rings but ends up going to her voice mail. Dropping the phone, I slide it back into my pocket.

"Nothing, huh?"

I frown. "Nope."

"Do you have a key? Or do we just—"

My attention is suddenly drawn from Wade to a female figure across the street. Standing beside the lamp post, her slight build and tall frame would be enough to draw my attention, but it's the red peacoat and oversize hood that makes me stop and stare.

"What is it?" Wade asks, turning his gaze to follow mine.

I chance a glance in his direction as I lean in and whisper, "See that woman over there? Does anything seem... odd about her? She's staring at us." A strange, anticipatory energy lingers in the air between us and it's like I'm drawn to her. Even if I didn't want to be, I'd be helpless to stop myself.

"Well, this is a small town." Wade chuckles. "She's probably checking to make sure we're not going to rob the place. Who knows...maybe your mom asked her to watch the house while she's away?"

"No, I don't think so. I've never seen her before," I mutter.

When I look back, the woman is gone from the lamp post. Instead, almost as if she teleported, she's at the other end of the block. Something inside me screams to follow her and without even stopping to tell Wade, I bound down the stairs and take off after her.

"Autumn, wait," Wade says, leaping from the doorstep and following me.

His feet crunch heavily in the snow behind me, but the only thing I can concentrate on is the woman in front of me. By the time I reach the end of the block, the woman's red coat disappears into the depths of the graveyard beyond and I pick up speed. I hit the interior of the graveyard, following the direction of the freshly made footsteps, searching for her red coat.

Without a doubt, there's something important about her—something I need to have answered. If only I can reach her...

"Autumn, wait. What if..." he reaches out, grabbing my hand and pulling me up short. "What if it's one of the Moirai?"

The word snaps me out of my trance like a slap in the face.

The Moirai...

I blink back my surprise, appalled that the thought hadn't even entered my mind. It should have been the first thing I thought. Yet the moment I saw her, any concern for myself vanished completely and all I knew was I needed to catch up with her.

"Oh, god," I say, pressing my fingertips to my mouth.

I spin around on the spot, searching for the woman, but her footsteps have disappeared on the snow, as if she led me here and vanished.

Beside us is a large statue of an angel. I've never noticed it before, in the many times I've visited this cemetery. Its face is tilted in anguish, tears carved across its marble face that look realistic in the dying sunlight. Its arms are outstretched, as if reaching for an offering. And there, dangling between the outstretched fingers, is another tattered red thread.

My eyes drift to the bronze plate at its feet. The words read: *I pledge my soul for your sins and ask God Almighty to remove their burden from you and place them with me to consume.*

I shudder at the imagery those words invoke.

Was she leading me here to atone for my sins? Or was she leading me to my death, in order to consume the mistakes of my ancestors?

CHAPTER 7
LIES

I stare at the red thread, unable to force my mind to make my body move. Instead, nervous energy rolls through me and I bend over, sucking in the crisp winter air as if my life depends on it. And I suppose it does.

"Are you okay, Dru?" Wade asks, kneeling beside me.

I shake my head. "No, I'm really not."

He rubs a circle on my back, leaning in close and providing the kind of comfort only he can offer.

"I would have followed her anywhere. Had you not snapped me out of it—who knows what would have happened?" I say, wiping at the side of my mouth to keep from being sick. Slowly, I stand up. The red thread flutters in the breeze, taunting me to free it from the stone fingertips.

Reaching out, I tug it free, and crumple it up in the palm of my hand.

"The Moirai are getting more relentless. It's a good thing we're here to get answers," Wade says, circling his gaze around the cemetery. "It's so strange. I have so many mixed feelings about this place."

I follow his stare to the columbarium where his grandfather's ashes would have resided—had they not risen as a revenant.

"Yeah, I know the feeling," I whisper.

"Come on. Let's get out of here," he says, wrapping his right arm around my shoulder. "Maybe your mom is home now."

Taking a deep breath, I pull out my phone to see if she's tried to get in touch. There are no messages. Scrunching my face, I put the phone back and trudge out of the cemetery.

This place used to be my favorite location in all of Mistwood Point. It was the one place where I felt safe. But now, it's as if my family legacy has triggered nothing but apprehension for it instead.

Our footsteps together are much slower than on the way into the graveyard. Wade slides his arm down, interlocking his hand in mine. For a few minutes, we walk in silence, listening to the sound of our shoes crunching on the snowy sidewalk.

The lamp posts have sprung to life, illuminating the walkways and guiding us back the way we came. The businesses on this edge of town begin to dwindle as it fades back into the more residential part. The majority of the houses now have lights on inside, where the businesses have turned dark.

As we pass by the small Mistwood Community Center, a grouping of about ten women and two men filter out the doors. They all chat among themselves as they pull their jackets in tighter against their chins when they meet the winter wind.

One guy hikes a gym bag up on his shoulder. "See you ladies on Tuesday. Have a good weekend, Ted," he says, waving. "Merry Christmas."

The rest of them look up, each responding with a slight wave of their own.

"Merry Christmas," most respond back.

I catch the eye of one of the women and she stops dead in the middle of her stride. "Autumn?"

"Mom?" I say, picking up my step to reach her.

"What are you two doing here? Did I know you were meant to be here tonight?" she asks, looking flustered.

I shake my head. "No, it was meant to be a surprise."

Her eyes widen, but she doesn't respond.

"So, surprise," Wade offers, doing jazz hands for effect.

Mom's hazel eyes flit from me to him as she shakes away her surprise and smiles. "Well, I'd give you both a hug, but I just got done with Pilates class. So, you might want to take a raincheck until after my shower."

"I didn't know you were taking Pilates," I say, surprised. She's always liked to work out, but doing anything that involves sweating around others is definitely new.

"Yeah, I thought it was time to see what all the hype was about," she chuckles, tipping her head toward the direction of her house. "Well, come on. Let's get to the house before we freeze out here."

We make our way down the sidewalk. The others in front of us start to disperse, disappearing into their relative houses.

"Does this mean you'll be staying for Christmas?" Mom finally asks, turning back to us.

I nod. "Yeah, that's the plan."

"Excellent. I was really hoping you'd change your mind," she grins, reaching out and squeezing my hand.

Wade nudges me with his shoulder.

I swallow hard, suddenly aware of how sweaty my palm feels. Clearing my throat, I say, "Mom... I have some stuff I need to talk to you about."

"What is it, sweetheart?" she asks, turning a questioning gaze my direction.

Scrunching my face, I point to the house a few hundred feet away. "Let's get inside first."

"Oh, boy. Is this going to be a big talk? You're not pregnant, are you?" Her hazel eyes widen as peers at us suspiciously. "Because the timing wouldn't be great."

Wade's shocked expression turns to me expectantly.

"No—that's not..." I say, shaking my head. Leave it to my mom to go someplace completely mundane rather than think about what I've recently been through with the estate. My insides tighten and I race ahead, taking the steps two at a time. I make it to the door first, pacing up and down the porch.

The two of them follow behind me, but as Mom takes out her keys, she narrows her gaze. "Hmmm..." she mutters. Unlocking the door, she swings it open, letting the two of us slide past her first.

"Okay, how about a cup of tea?" Mom says, dropping her keys on the entryway table. "Wade, you like British tea, right?"

"That would be great," he nods, following her.

I stand in the middle of the small entryway, trying to

settle my flyaway heart. My eyes drift along the banister to the stairs leading up and I sigh.

Pregnant. I wish that's all this was.

Shaking my head, I follow them.

With the kettle in hand, Mom walks to the sink, filling it up. Wade takes a seat at the breakfast bar, clasping his hands out in front of him as he waits.

"We can order pizza. How does Hawaiian sound?" Mom asks as she sets the kettle on the stove.

My forehead creases, but I nod. "Yeah, that'll be great."

Wade seconds the response with an adamant nod.

Mom grabs three mugs from the dishwasher and sets them down on the counter. "Okay, so what is it you want to talk about, then?"

Part of me would like nothing more than to sit down next to Wade, but the other part of me is too agitated to sit still. Instead, I opt for pacing behind him.

"Mom, you and Dad were divorced, right?" I blurt out. The moment the words leave my lips, I turn to face her, holding my breath. I watch her every movement and micro-expression as if they are the only things that will lead me to the truth.

The question does as I expected. She pauses, wide-eyed and mouth slightly agape. Then, her eyes flutter frantically, as she turns to check on the kettle.

"Mom?"

I glance at Wade, whose expression tells me everything I need to know.

She places her hands on the oven's handle, dropping her chin to her chest. "It's not that we were keeping things..."

Releasing my held breath, I reach for the other stool and take a seat.

Mom turns around, her sorrowful gaze meeting mine. She holds it for a moment, but no more words escape her lips.

Tears brim in my eyes and I shake my head. "Mom... how could you keep that from me?"

Wade's hand is suddenly on my back, his warm palm rubbing circles against the space between my shoulders.

Her voice is barely a whisper. "We thought it would be easier on you. Help you live a more...normal life."

"Normal? You call any of this normal?" I sputter. "Dad's dead. I'm being hunted by the literal Fates. And until a little over a year ago, I had no idea there was anything supernatural about me. But you knew—you knew all of this."

I lean forward, reaching into my back pocket. Pulling out the letter from my dad, I slap it on the counter between us.

Mom's forehead creases. "What's this?"

"A letter from Dad," I say, sliding it over to her.

She swallows hard, but takes a step forward, reaching for the envelope. Removing the letter, she shoots us one last confused glance before reading his words.

I already know what's said in there. I read it when I found his journal, thanks to Abigail. He was going after the Moirai to protect me—and he wanted her to know he'd do everything he could to keep me safe.

Yeah, that went well.

Tears fill her eyes and she clutches at the necklace dangling in front of her throat.

"Did you still love him?" I say, swiping at my own tears falling across my cheeks.

Her expression is nothing more than pure agony, and my heart rips in two. "More than anything," she whispers.

"Then why? Why did you leave him?" I demand. "Who does that sort of thing? Was it because of me?"

"Autumn, you have to understand..." she begins, trying to sound reasonable, despite the tears brimming in her eyes. She looks between Wade and me as if searching for the best way to deliver the news. Or maybe just hoping he'd help her find a way to calm me down.

"Mom, enough of the bullshit. Just tell me what the hell is going on. Why was Blackwood Manor willed to you? And why did I have to find out about you and dad from some goddamn lawyer? What in the hell could possibly be the reason for keeping me in the dark about all of this?" I spit.

"We had to—" she fires back. As soon as the words leave her lips, her eyes widen and she presses her fingertips against her mouth.

I narrow my gaze. "You had to?"

Mom sighs, setting down the letter on the counter. "I'm sorry, Autumn. You deserve to know the full story. I just don't know if—"

"Mom, we're down to the wire here. Those signs Dad talks about in the letter," I say, pressing my index finger into the crumpled paper. "They're happening to me now. Everywhere I go. The mall, the manor, the cemetery here in Mistwood. I don't know how long I have. I don't know how to stop this when he couldn't even put an end to it. What I *do* know is my entire childhood has been a lie and

I need some damn answers. Otherwise I'm going to end up like the rest of the Blackwood family—*dead*."

Mom gasps, pressing her fist against her heart. Her head twitches back and forth, clearly shaken by my words. Part of me is actually pleased that they had such an impact.

"I really tried to keep you safe. We both did. But it's clear that's no longer up to me." She stifles a sob. "You're right. I've been keeping so much from you. It's time I tell you everything."

CHAPTER 8
FAMILY MATTERS

Mom's face is a mixture of emotions as she paces from one end of the small kitchen to the other. Both Wade and I watch her closely, anticipating what she might say. There are so many secrets she could be holding onto. Neither of us say a word; we just wait for her to be ready to reveal whatever information she's ready to share.

After a minute, she stops moving, leans against the sink, and places her hands on the counter behind her. "Last year, we talked a little bit about things, Autumn. Like what happened when you went missing. But you hung up before we could *really talk*." Her eyes flick up to me, holding my gaze for a moment. "Not that I'm blaming you at all. Things between us have been so strained because of... Well, it is what it is. However, I knew"—her eyelashes flutter across her cheeks as she looks down—"that day on the phone, I knew something was going on. Something horrible. I could *feel* it."

Goosebumps flash across the back of my arms and my

eyebrows tug in. Mom has always been incredibly perceptive. Even as a kid I could barely get away with a white lie about eating all of my vegetables without her finding the place I'd dumped them outside. But the way her words linger in the air between us, there's something much more potent than simply a mother's sense.

She continues, "There's so much... I'm not sure where to start in all of this."

"Start at the beginning," Wade offers in his soothing way.

Her gaze rises, landing on him momentarily. A question lingers there, but she nods. "The beginning... That's a place I haven't cared to visit for quite some time." Her eyes dart back and forth with her thoughts as she works to pull the pieces together. "Autumn, all this time, you must be wondering why I despised the supernatural world so much. Especially knowing what you know now about your gifts...and your father's."

My lips press into a thin line, and I nod. She already knows these questions have lingered in my mind. I've even voiced them to her.

"I have lived in the world of the supernatural far longer than you realize. Far longer than you can perhaps comprehend," she says, dropping her gaze again to the floor.

Alarm bells go off inside my head and I can't help but push the stool back and stand up. "What do you mean?"

Her sorrowful hazel eyes meet mine and her eyebrows upturn in the middle. She holds her breath and releases it, as if the breath itself was a heavy burden to carry. "Autumn, in times past, before supernatural beings were accepted the way they are, we were often considered to be gods. Particularly those of us who defy the traditional roles of death."

My brain seizes up and it's my turn to be flustered. I take another step back from the bar. "*Us?*"

Wade scoots his own stool back, standing up and preparing to get between us, if need be. His silver eyes dart between us, as if trying to decide who will make the first move.

"Yes, *us*," she says, swallowing hard. "I'm sorry, sweet girl. In another life, I was so excited to show you the beauty in our powers. But..."

"*Us?*" I repeat, my hands flying to my hair as I pull at the red strands. This can't be happening. There's no way my mom is a supernatural being. No possible way. I drop my hands, twisting back to her and demand, "If you have powers, what are they? What are you? Prove it."

"I have many powers. They've developed through the ages," she whispers.

I close my eyes, trying to process her words. *Ages?*

"Are you saying you're one of the old gods?" Wade asks, somehow managing to break the chaos clouding my mind and asking a question buried in my thoughts.

My head snaps up just in time to see her flinch.

"No..." I say, raising my hands and backing away. "No. Just, no. You can't be. I've lived with you my whole life. You like your sleep. You hate to argue. You eat eggs, drink protein shakes, and work out. You do Pilates, for crying out loud. You can't—"

Looking up from beneath her eyebrows, she says, "I've gone by many names in my lifetime. But the one that stuck in the pages of history is *Hecate*. I can't say it's my favorite."

My mouth drops open and my mind goes completely blank. It's like the entire world I live in, everything about it, has been nothing but one big, fat lie.

For the first time, Mom walks around the counter that was separating us. Wade takes a protective step forward, but the look on my mother's face makes him step back.

"Autumn, you have to know, there are so many times I wanted to tell you. To explain why you had certain gifts for things, like accidentally resurrecting the neighbor's cat when you were nine and bringing birds who hit the window back to life. Instead, I had to pretend to ignore them—write them off as completely normal occurrences. It's gone against every instinct I have to keep silent, but I had to protect you. That's been my priority since—"

"Gifts? Ignore them? I don't remember any of that. Until I went to live at Dad's, I didn't even know I had supernatural gifts," I sputter.

Mom shakes her head, placing her hands on my shoulders. "That's not true."

"Then why don't I remember?" I fire back.

"Because I made sure you didn't," she whispers, locking eyes with me. "Your memories around those events needed to be a blank slate or the Moirai would sense your growing power; your connection to the forces of life and death. They'd know you were still alive and they'd look for a way to take you from me."

"But they're Fate," Wade sputters. "They create the fabric of reality for every single life. Wouldn't her thread tell them she's still alive? Hell, the fact that she *is* alive— wouldn't that technically be their doing?"

"I don't know," Mom whispers, shooting a sideways glance toward Wade.

An absurd laugh bursts from my chest. "You don't know? You're a friggin' goddess and you don't know?"

Mom makes a face as she turns to me. "First of all, I'm no different from you or any other supernatural being. I just live longer. That's all. Secondly, what I do know is that the signs—the red threads—they stopped appearing when you vanished. They didn't start back up when you reappeared, either. What you did, resurrecting yourself, it should have been *impossible*. So we figured perhaps the Moirai didn't know you'd returned. We took that chance and it worked well for us while we searched for answers."

Wade's eyes are wide as he looks between the two of us.

"If you've been wiping my memory anyway, why did we have to leave? Why did you take us from Dad? Ugh, none of this makes sense," I say, slamming my hand on the table in frustration.

"The manor is at the center of a vortex. Its energy draws in the supernatural, but also opens the veil between the dead and the living. Keeping you there—it was too obvious. They'd find you, even if I kept your memory clean," she says, breathing heavy as she fights back tears. "God, Autumn. I wanted to stay there. You have no idea how much I wanted to stay."

"Then why didn't Dad come with us? You could have protected—"

"He was the cursed one, just like you. Only, he didn't have the luxury you did," Mom says, cutting me off.

"Luxury? You call dying a luxury?" I spit.

"Call it what you will, then. Loophole. Whatever. Your father knew the only way to stop the Moirai was to find a way to break the curse. So, that's what we did. Both of us have spent the better part of a decade hunting for information. Searching the ends of reality for a way to stop whatever fate may come our way. Clearly, it wasn't enough," she whispers. Tears tumble from her cheeks and she turns away from me, wiping at her face.

"Autumn's dad left her a small decorative box in the will. The executor didn't seem to know what it was, just that she was meant to have it. Do you know what it's for?" Wade asks, obviously thinking more clearly than either of us.

Mom turns back, her face full of confusion. "A box? No. What does it look like?"

"I can go grab it. We brought it with us," Wade offers, making his way to the front door.

The two of us stand in silence, staring at each other as if it's the first time we've really ever seen one another for who we are. Maybe it is.

After a moment, Wade comes back in, carrying a backpack and pulling two suitcases. He leaves the suitcases beside the stairs, but makes his way back to us with the backpack over his shoulder. When he reaches the table, he shrugs it off and opens it wide.

"Here, Autumn," he says, handing the box to me.

I clutch the wooden artifact close, pressing my fingertips against the rounded edges of the carvings. When I look up into Mom's curious face, I extend my arms and place the box in her hands.

She looks at it closely, twisting and turning the box from one way to the next, until she's looked the whole thing over. "I've never seen this before, but it's incredibly powerful. The sigils on here alone..."

"That's what Abigail said," I mutter, fighting the urge

to be sick. The nausea and anxiety swirl from my stomach, up to my throat, making me feel both dizzy and queasy at the same time. "That it was powerful."

Her eyes dart up to meet mine. "You speak to Abigail?"

I nod, refusing to go into more details with her right now. "What are the sigils?"

She blinks away her surprise, returning her gaze to the box. "See here?" Tipping the box so I can look at the corners, she taps her finger on one particular symbol. Enclosed in a circle, it looks like a model of the solar system in stick-figure form. "This one is a sigil for protection. But what it's protecting, I'm not sure."

Apprehension and fear consume my thoughts, and I can't help but worry about the reasons behind willing the box to me.

"Do you think it's dangerous?" I blurt out, looking at it with fresh wariness.

She continues to rotate the box in her hands. "I'm not certain. I'd have to research some of the writing. It's old."

Inhaling deeply, I suddenly feel like I'm going to be sick again. The information coming at me is too much and I need to find a way to control my anxiety in peace.

"You know, I'm not feeling..." I begin, trying to breathe through a new wave of nausea. "I think I need a few minutes to clear my head." Without waiting for either of them to respond, I make my way from the kitchen, walking down the hallway toward the bathroom.

I press my right hand along the wall, trying to keep myself upright as I close the door behind me. Looking in the mirror, I'm horrified at my complexion. My skin is waxy, and my eyes have lost their usual luster.

Before I can admonish myself any further, I run over to

the toilet, emptying the contents of my stomach. When it's all over and I'm dry-heaving, I lean back, resting my head against the cool wall. My eyes drift to the nearly empty toilet roll and out of reflex, I reach forward, opening the cupboard under the sink. I grab the toilet paper, but my eyes rest on the feminine hygiene products sitting beside it. They were mine from before I moved—remnants of my time here.

I wipe the side of my mouth, my hand sliding from there to my abdomen. I don't remember the last time I had my period. Things have been an intense blur these past few weeks, but the last time I remember dealing with it was just after Halloween. Surely, I should have had it by now?

My mom's question from earlier comes flooding back and a fresh wave of nausea makes me return to the toilet bowl and heave.

This can't be happening... Not now, not with every-thing going on.

I can't be...*pregnant*. Can I?

CHAPTER 9
OUT IN THE OPEN

I don't even know why I tried to sleep.

It's almost laughable, if I wasn't on the verge of breaking down completely. My entire world is splitting apart and even if I found solid ground, there's no guarantee it would hold.

No matter what I do, I can't stop thinking about the possibility of being pregnant. And even when I do manage to drift for a split second, or lapse on this new obsession, my thoughts snap right back to my mom.

How in the hell could she be a supernatural? And not just any supernatural, either—one that's been around so long she was considered a goddess before we understood that some people were...*different*.

What does that mean? What powers does she truly have? We barely had time to get into it, but I don't think I could have taken on any more right now. My whole life— everything I thought I knew about my family, my mom—it was all a lie.

I'm not sure I know how to deal with that.

In fact, I don't get any of it. If she's been around as long as she implied, why would she give everything up to pretend she was human? The things she's seen—the places she's been. If that were me, I don't know that I could give it up so easily. Even if I wanted to protect my child.

The concept is just too foreign.

I roll over, trying not to wake up Wade. I haven't found a way to voice my suspicions about my sickness, and I don't want to worry him if it's really just anxiety. Yet, even as I think that, I know better. There's a strange, horrifying realization settling into the back of my mind—maybe my gut—that tells me I need to be sure.

But if it's true, it couldn't be worse timing. The last thing either of us needs is to bring a child into the mix of a family curse brought on by the Fates.

My heartbeat quickens and I have to take slow deliberate breaths to settle my shallow, rapid inhalations.

If I am pregnant, what will happen to the child? Wade might be expelled from the Angel of Death legacy, but would his child? Would it skip his generation and simply fall onto our offspring? And if so—what would that mean to the Moirai? Would that connection protect him or her? Or would they still claim that child as a Blackwood? If they did end our child's life, would that mean the human life has been forfeit but the baby still gets to ascend as an angel? Or would both of our bloodlines die out?

The possibilities make my stomach roll and I fight the urge to sit up in bed or race to the bathroom. I spend the next few hours, drifting in and out of an uncomfortable, restless sleep.

By the time morning comes, I barely feel as though I've fallen asleep at all. My mind is instantly on the possible pregnancy and the need to know for sure. For whatever reason, it feels like the one thing in this whole crazy, mixed-up life I can control. Even if that control is only an illusion.

"I think I'm going to take a walk, if that's okay," I announce as I bring my breakfast plate to the sink. If I can get out, I can walk down to the drugstore and get a pregnancy test.

Both Wade and my mom look up at me as if I've managed to grow horns on the top of my head.

"What?" I ask defensively.

"Well, it's just—you haven't said two words this morning," Wade says, trying to smooth out his face. "It was just an abrupt shift."

I run my fingertips across my forehead, nodding to myself. "Yeah, sorry. Just in my head a bit. Lots to mull over, you know? That's why I thought a walk might do me some good."

"Do you want me to go with you?" Wade asks, getting up from his seat.

I shake my head, reaching out for him. "No, stay. Sit. It's okay. I need a few minutes."

His expression turns doubtful. "Do you really think you should be out on the streets alone? I mean, after what happened last night with the woman..."

Shit, I hadn't thought of that. Of all the things circling my brain at this particular moment, the woman and her connection to the Moirai were pushed further to the recesses of my mind. Which is bizarre in its own way, since the Moirai have been the only thing on my mind for weeks.

"I'll go with her. I think we need a little time to talk,"

Mom says, shifting back her chair and standing up. "Wade, would you mind taking a look at the television? It hasn't connected to the Blu-ray player in ages and I'd love to bust out our stash of Christmas films tonight. It's a Christmas Eve tradition in this house."

Wade shifts his gaze from my mom back to me, a silent question lingering in his eyes.

Nodding my head, I say, "It's okay. She's right, we have a lot to talk about. Besides, I'd be useless with the Blu-ray thing." I shoot him a smile, but I'm not certain it was very convincing.

His eyes narrow as he stands up and rests his hands on my arms. Looking deep into my eyes, he finally says, "Take your phone and if anything strange happens—"

I step forward, placing a kiss on his lips. "You'll be the first I call."

He watches me for a moment, but finally nods and turns to my mom. "All right, Andrea. Would you mind showing me this Blu-ray player you speak of?"

The two of them wander into the living room as she shows him the outdated electronic equipment. With the exception of watching Buffy reruns when I was younger, neither of us really spent much time watching television. It's no wonder the thing isn't working right.

After fifteen minutes of explanation and discussion, Wade is on the floor following cables and Mom walks over to me.

"Ready?" she asks, her voice soft.

I nod, reaching to grab my coat from the rack. She does the same and shrugs into it.

"We'll be back soon," I call out, putting my coat on. "Promise."

Wade stands up and brushes off his knees. In four huge strides he stands in front of me. Without a word, he places his hands on either side of my face and bends forward. His lips press down on mine, making my skin tingle and my cheeks flush.

"You better," he whispers, as he takes a step.

Mom turns away, reaching for the door handle and trying to pretend she didn't witness any of that.

I grin, standing up on my toes and brushing my lips one last time against his.

Without another word, Mom opens the door and we walk out into the blustery cold. Large snowflakes drift through the air, blanketing the ground as they sparkle in the sunlight trying to peek through in places. I zip my coat up to my chin and shove my hands into my pockets.

We walk down the sidewalk in silence, just watching the snow fall.

After a few minutes, Mom turns to me and says, "Autumn, there were so many times I wanted to tell you everything. I miss how things were with us before."

I quirk an eyebrow. "Before?"

She nods. "Before your accident. Everything was out in the open. You were in training with your dad. Abigail was there, too. Though your dad couldn't be certain. You talked about a woman being there."

I face my gaze forward, concentrating on the snow-covered sidewalk. "I don't remember any of that."

"I know," she sighs. "I'm sorry, sweetheart. The memories, they may come back. I just don't know for sure."

"It doesn't matter now," I say, biting the side of my lip.

She tips her chin in acknowledgment. "I suppose you're right."

"So, *Hecate*, huh?" I say, shaking my head. "I don't remember all the details about the mythologies. Had I known, I would have paid closer attention."

Mom chuckles. "Mythologies don't always get things right."

"But you're immortal?" I say, shooting her a sideways glance.

Her forehead creases and she shrugs. "Honestly, I don't know. The longer I've been around, the more I notice signs of aging."

"What do you mean?"

"I don't know. I'm finally getting gray hair?" she laughs. "Pretty sure that's *all you*."

I roll my eyes and she nudges me with her shoulder.

My head still can't wrap around the idea of my mother being so old. Or supernatural.

"If you're immor—really, *really* old," I say, narrowing my gaze and smirking at her, "could I have inherited that gene? Would that explain how I didn't drown? Maybe that's what really happened. Maybe I didn't resurrect myself at all?"

The idea that maybe I would have a longer-than-normal life suddenly flares against my imagination. Would that protect me against the Moirai?

But if it was the case, would I want to live so long? Or would that be painful to watch those you love continue to leave you? Had Wade still been next in line to become an Angel of Death, perhaps...

Mom's expression turns thoughtful and she shakes her head. "I don't think so, sweetie. It took me half a century to reach what looked like age ten. Your aging process has been pretty typical."

I can't help but frown. For a brief moment, the idea had balanced on the edge of being appealing.

"We do share some commonalities, though," Mom says, her forehead furrowing.

"Like what?"

"Well, for starters, I can also communicate with the dead. And I love graveyards, too. But I can see them for what they are—gateways into the realm of the eternal," she says, keeping her voice low as we approach a family building a snowman in their yard.

We're closer now to the drugstore and I need to find a way to break away from her for a moment to get what I need inside.

My eyebrows flick upward and I exhale slowly. "I don't know what to say to that."

"It's why your father and I were attracted to one another, I think. We shared so much in common—so much I didn't think I'd ever share with anyone. The gifts we share aren't very common. In fact, I'd wager..." she pauses, as if choosing her words carefully. After a moment, she sighs and says, "Wade is special, too, isn't he?"

I stop walking and twist to look at her, unsure what to tell her. "He used to be," I finally admit.

"Used to be?" Mom asks, her eyes narrowing.

"Yeah, it's complicated."

"Try me. I'm pretty sure I can keep up," Mom says, reaching out and touching my elbow.

I swallow hard, turning from her for a moment. Do I tell her everything? That he was expelled for loving me? That it's my fault he'll never be supernatural, never have powers...

Sighing, I say, "The powers he would have gained were

stripped from him. But you're right. He was meant to be an Angel of Death."

Mom takes a step back, eyes wide. It clearly wasn't what she had been anticipating.

"An Angel of Death? Are you certain?" she whispers.

"Very." I nod.

She shakes her head, stepping away and pacing. "And he was stripped of his birthright, you say? How did this happen?"

"His father. He was given a mark that expelled him from the club, I guess." I shift uncomfortably to one foot, eyeing the drug store a block away.

Her eyebrows tug in and she taps her lips with the tip of her finger.

"What is it?" I ask.

Mom's hazel gaze switches to me and she says, "Maybe nothing. But I'd like to look at this mark. Do you think he'd let me see it?"

I shrug. "Probably."

She nods, clearly lost in her own thoughts.

"Mom, I—uh, forgot my toothbrush. I'm going to run into the drugstore quick and pick up a new one. I'll be right back," I say, trying to make a quick getaway while she's thinking.

"Oh, okay," she says, blinking back her inner monologue. "I'll come, too. I could use some more shampoo."

I pull up short, shaking my head. "I can get it for you. Do you use the same stuff as always?"

Mom's eyes narrow and she smirks. "Yes, but I can grab my own stuff."

The suspicion in her eyes makes me shift gears. "Suit

yourself," I say, feigning nonchalance. "I was just trying to be helpful."

"Hmmm," she mutters, following me anyway.

My heartbeat thumps awkwardly as I pull back the door and step inside. It's not an overly large store, so keeping things under wraps is going to be difficult. The feminine products are only an aisle over from the shampoo.

I make my way over to the small gift section, pretending to eye the knickknacks and trinkets. Predictably, Mom follows me, checking out the small rack of sweatshirts that say "Mistwood Point" on them.

"Do you need a sweatshirt to remind you of me?" she chuckles, holding a purple one out in front of her. She closes one eye, trying to match it up with my frame.

"Sure," I say, smiling. "That was my devious plan. Get you in the store so you can buy me clothes."

She quirks an eyebrow. "I thought it might be."

I shake my head. "I'm going to grab that toothbrush."

I meander away from her, watching her dig through the other racks of clothing. As quickly as I can, I grab a toothbrush. I don't even look at it; the kind doesn't matter—it's just a prop.

Shooting another glance down the aisle to locate her whereabouts, I catch a glimpse of her back as she eyes the jewelry display. She's always loved the natural stone necklaces and bracelets they have here.

Slipping behind the aisle, I make my way to the feminine products section, scanning quickly for the pregnancy tests. I find them on the bottom shelf. Scanning them quickly, I pluck the first one that catches my eye.

99.9% accurate, it reads in the bright-yellow starburst. That'll do.

There's no sight of my mom as I sneak my way to checkout with my contraband in hand. She's probably grabbing her shampoo, so I have to be fast.

I slide my items on the checkout, standing on my toes to hunt for the pharmacist assistant, who's usually right there and waiting. Rocking back and forth on my feet, I lean as far across the counter as I dare.

Thankfully, she looks up from whatever prescription she must have been filling.

"Be there in just a second, dear," she says as she finishes up counting.

I look again over my shoulder, eyes wide, as I try to locate my mother. My fingertips tap the side of the counter as I try to dispel my impatience.

The woman sets aside the prescription and walks over to the register with a smile.

"Ah, Autumn. I thought that was you," she says as she gets closer.

"Yep," I say, trying not to bounce up and down. I shove the items across the counter to her.

She grabs the toothbrush first, scanning it. My insides are screaming at her to hurry up. Relief floods through me as she reaches for the pregnancy test. Thankfully, the woman doesn't say a word. She just quirks an eyebrow and presses her lips into a thin line.

The register dings loudly as she scans it and sets it aside. I hold my breath as she reaches for a bag.

"Is that a pregnancy test?" Mom says from directly over my shoulder.

CHAPTER 10
PUT TO THE TEST

I twist around, meeting my mom's expectant gaze. Her eyes sparkle with a strange glow that makes the green flecks in her irises pulsate. How have I never noticed that before now? She holds my stare, but after a moment, the corner of her mouth twitches into a half-smile. In the simple gesture, my lips part for me to say something, but I end up snapping them shut.

"You don't need that test. I could tell from the moment you walked into the house," Mom says, setting her shampoo on the counter behind me as she turns to the pharmacy clerk. "Hi, Terri. How's your mom doing?"

"Good, Mrs. Blackwood," Terri says, tipping her chin. "Want me to ring these all up together?"

"Yep, sounds good," Mom says, ushering me aside with a swipe of her arm.

I stand there, staring at her as she takes charge with the sale and manages everything else in complete stride. Me, on the other hand... Can a person forget how to think?

Blinking away my shock, I take another step back from the counter. I practically bump into the small display of sunglasses as I give Mom room to pay for everything because I lost all sense to stop her.

After a few more quiet words with Terri, she turns back to me. "Ready to head home?"

I nod, still unable to form words just yet. One word rattles around inside my head.

Pregnant.

I follow Mom outside, barely aware of my surroundings, let alone how to put one foot in front of the other.

Mom pulls me aside when we hit the sidewalk. "He really loves you, you know. It's pretty evident in the way he kissed you before we left."

I stare back at her, nodding. "Yeah."

"Do you love him?" she asks, tilting her head to the side and taking in my every movement.

My shoulders release and I exhale. "More than anything."

Her face softens and she chuckles under her breath. "That'll change when the little one arrives. Not that you'll love him any less, mind you. But your capacity to love just gets so much bigger. Bigger than you ever thought possible. In fact, so much so that it can be downright scary."

"More scary than being hunted by fate?" I sputter. They're the first words that come to mind, but they're my truth at this moment.

She raises her hand, pressing her thumb against my chin. "Not quite, but damn close."

My face must betray me because she sets the bag of stuff on the snow-covered bench outside the drugstore, then pulls me to her. After a few moments, she whispers,

"We will find a way out of this. I promise you that." I shoot her a doubtful glance and she sighs. "He'll make a good dad, you know."

"Yeah, if we ever get that far." A smile flits across my face and tears well in my eyes. I pull back to wipe them away. "Are you sure? I mean about me? About this?" I ask, letting my hands fall to my abdomen.

Mom's eyes crease and she says, "It's one of my specialties. We might share a lot in common when it comes to death and the afterlife, sweetheart. But there's actually a fine line between birth and death. You just have to know where to look."

Anxiety wells up inside my chest and I swallow hard. "This is not a good time."

"It's never a good time, Autumn. Kids are scary shit," she chuckles. "But you can't fear living just because you know one day all of this will end. The end comes for most of us someday. No, I don't care if you're twenty-two or being chased by the Moirai. Take it from me. Running in fear means you end up missing the point of life entirely," she says, frowning.

"Are you talking about you and Dad?" I ask, narrowing my eyes.

Her forehead creases. "Had I known you would have ended up right in the middle of all of this anyway, I don't think I would have made the same choices. I would have insisted we take a different path."

"You have no idea how much I wish you had," I whisper, thinking of all the lost time with Dad—with the manor. With my gifts. Maybe having learned about them and the Moirai earlier would have been what we needed to overcome them.

What if now it's too late?

"Mom, I can't bring a baby in the middle of all of this," I say, suddenly overwhelmed by the emotions clawing at my insides. "What in the hell am I going to do? We have to stop the Moirai—"

"Listen to me," she says, gripping me by my shoulders. "We will find a way out of this. All of us, *together*."

I nod frantically, hoping the truth in her words somehow finds a way into my soul, because right now, I'm feeling utterly helpless and alone. Raising my hand to my mouth, I sputter, "Oh, my god. Wade. How am I going to tell Wade?"

"Just relax. Sit with this a bit. Take that test, if you think it will make it easier. Then, wrap it up as a present and give it to him for Christmas," Mom says, her expression thoughtful.

I glare at her from under my eyebrows. "That's the cheesiest thing you've ever said to me."

"And yet, I bet you don't have a better plan." She grins back.

I run my hand down my face.

"You'll be fine, sweetheart. Whatever you choose—however you decide to tell him—it will be perfect." She reaches past me, picking up the bag and facing my body toward the house.

We walk back, listening to the sound of our feet crunching in the snow. The closer we get, I'm a bundle of nerves as I try to figure out the best way to tell Wade. Do I do what Mom suggested, as corny as it is? Or do I find some other way to tell him?

What will he say? What will he think?

God, we never talked about this—any of it. Kids,

marriage. It's almost as if neither one of us could foresee a future where all of that existed.

I shudder at the thought, pulling my coat in tighter.

When we reach the house, I'm practically ready to head back in the other direction. Mom must sense my apprehension, too. As we walk inside, her gaze floats around the room to find Wade. When they land on him sitting on the couch, she hands me the bag and says, "Hey sweetie, can you bring the shampoo and toothbrush to the bathroom for me? Then, let's get started on Christmas dinner. Wade, did you want to help, too?"

She walks away from me, allowing me the excuse to run to the bathroom while she occupies Wade with our next Christmas task.

I rush down to the bathroom, my nerves once again on high alert. For whatever reason, I'm more terrified to know if Mom is right than anything else. Give me the Moirai—let me face fate and death. Just please, don't let me be pregnant. I can't be...

Closing the door behind me, I make sure to flick the lock. I pull the toothbrush and shampoo out, placing them in plain sight in case Wade comes in later. I also carefully remove the pregnancy test and set it on the counter as gingerly as possible. Then, I stare at it as if it might catch fire any second.

My heart throbs, making my hands sweat. I wipe them on my jeans and reach for the box. Without allowing time to talk myself out of it, I rip the box open and pull out the test. The small plastic stick is one of the most intimidating tools I've ever seen—and that's saying something. I have a mysterious, magic box in my possession, after all.

My hand shakes and I flip the box over, bending in to

read the instructions. Because there's no way I'm screwing this up.

I follow the instructions to the letter, then sit down on the edge of the bathtub to wait. I hold my breath, watching the second hand tick forward from the small clock on the countertop. When the time is up, I stare forward, unable to bring myself to look over the results just yet.

"Autumn—are you okay?" Wade calls out from the hall-way, making me jump.

I stand up, clutching at my heart. "Yeah, I'm fine. I'll be out in a minute."

"Were you sick again?" he asks, his voice close—clearly on the other side of the door.

"No, not at all. Just needed the bathroom," I sputter, picking up the box and instructions so I can toss them into the bin. "I'll be out in a second."

"Okay, your mom is starting on the turkey. She goes all out for this Christmas stuff, huh?" He chuckles.

"Yeah," I mutter, trying to calm my breathing down as I stare at the back of the door.

When I hear his footsteps echo away, I lean against the counter, staring one last time in the mirror before casting my gaze to the test.

Now or never.

I glance down. There are two pink lines clear across the little window.

Tears swell in my eyes and a sob escapes my lips.

Pregnant.

Oh, my god, I'm pregnant.

I inhale deeply, staring at the test. There's no turning back. We have more than just ourselves to protect now.

Without thinking, I reach forward, shoving the test into my front pocket. Suddenly, the idea of wrapping it up and giving it to him for Christmas doesn't seem so ludicrous after all.

I'll find a way to sneak away after dinner's in the oven so I can wrap it. I don't know how he'll react, but one way or another, he'll know soon enough.

I open the door, walking down the hallway and into the kitchen. Mom's at the sink, washing her hands. On top of the stove is the prepared turkey, ready to be placed in the oven. She's decked it all out with citrus fruits and onions.

Wade grins, grabbing an olive from one of the small bowls on the counter. "Hey there, beautiful."

"Hey," I say, walking over to him.

Mom turns around, catching my eye. She quirks an eyebrow—her silent question coming across loud and clear. I tip my chin slightly in return. The smile on her face broadens and she walks to the stove, pulling open the oven door.

"Well, I don't know about you two, but I'm looking forward to a proper turkey dinner," she says, placing the beastly pan inside.

"I'm just excited to be a part of a family dinner," Wade says, smiling softly.

Instinctively, I place my hand on his back, rubbing it back and forth. I'd forgotten how little family experiences he's had. He was on the street since he was fifteen—just after his dad died. With his mom out of the picture, what did his holidays look like? God, they must have been so sad.

Suddenly, the idea of being pregnant takes on a new

meaning. It's the exact thing Wade's always been searching for. And here I am, scared to death of it being true.

Mom's right. This might not be perfect timing, but it might still be perfect.

A strange rush of excitement flows through me and I reach for the test in my pocket.

"Do you smell that?" Wade says, scrunching up his nose.

I raise my nose, sniffing into the air. All I can smell is the turkey cooking in the next room.

"What do you smell?" I ask.

He frowns, his eyes distant as he shudders. "It's like... something's burning."

Mom chuckles. "Well, I know you haven't eaten here often, but I assure you, I know how to cook a turkey."

Wade shakes his head. "No, it's not that. It's something else. Something horrible. Like burnt hair and flesh."

My eyes widen as I look around the room. The panic button inside me instantly goes off. "Are you sure? I don't smell anything like—"

Suddenly, Wade clutches at his chest and arches backward on his stool. Before I can stop him, he twists back, falling from the stool and crashing to the floor.

CHAPTER 11
BREATHE

Before I even reach Wade, Mom is on the phone behind me, sputtering out words like "ambulance" and "hurry."

I scramble off of my stool, dropping to my knees beside him. "Wade," I cry out, pressing my hands to his shoulders.

He groans in agony, clutching at his chest as the rest of his body writhes on the tiles.

"I don't understand. How can I help you? What's happening?" My words tumble out in a higher octave as I try to calm him down, but I don't know how to do that when I can't calm myself.

He groans incomprehensibly, and his silver eyes widen, begging me to stop whatever's tormenting him. Reaching up with his left hand, he tugs at his t-shirt collar, exposing the upper part of his clavicle and chest. The mark left by his father is clearly evident, but dark spidery lines emanate from the jagged circle, spreading outward across his chest and snaking their way up his neck.

Out of shock and terror, I pull my hands back. "Oh, my god, what is that?"

Still clutching the phone to her ear, Mom drops down beside me. She pulls back the fabric from Wade's chest, eyeing the mark and its new infection with the expression of a surgeon.

"Is this the mark he was given?" she asks, turning her concerned gaze on me.

I nod frantically. "But it shouldn't look like this. There's something wrong."

Wade's body clenches forward, and he gropes again at his chest.

"Do you smell that?" he repeats, trying to reach out for me. His pupils are fully dilated and wild with panic.

I press my hand to his forehead, trying to soothe him. "No, Wade. I don't smell anything." Turning to Mom, she meets my gaze with uneasiness clear in her eyes.

Setting the phone down on the counter, she presses her hands to his chest and closes her eyes. I hold my breath, watching her.

After a moment, she releases her hands and sighs. "I don't know what this is. It's obviously a reaction to the mark—but I'm not sure what's caused it. The ambulance is on its way. Hopefully, the doctors can find more to go on."

"No, no doctors," Wade sputters, shaking his head.

"Honey, you're not dying on my kitchen floor," Mom says, pressing his head back down to the tile. "Now, just relax for a minute, okay?"

"Dying?" I cry.

Mom shifts her hazel eyes to me, holding my gaze for the longest minute of my life. Finally she says, "Something is very, very wrong here. He's treading a thin line... Can't you sense it?"

My pulse skyrockets and tears swell in my eyes. "No— he doesn't even know..." I shake my head. "Absolutely not. Do you hear me, Wade. You stay with me."

Suddenly, there's a booming on the front door and Mom is on her feet, racing to open it.

Two men the size of tanks rush in with a stretcher in between them. As they enter, they drop the stretcher and it clangs loudly on the tiles. One of them kneels on the floor beside me while the other one places a gentle hand on my shoulder. He asks me something, but I have no idea what. All I know is I'm suddenly being tugged to my feet.

I reach out for Wade, not wanting to leave his side. Tears stream down my cheeks and I'm acutely aware that my own words are incoherent.

Mom wraps her arms around me, holding me close as the two men assess Wade on the cold, gray tile. Her presence radiates, and I can't help but lean into it. I raise a trembling hand to my mouth, trying to squelch the terror rising in the back in my throat.

The first man cuts open Wade's shirt, revealing the extent of the mark and its infection. The dark tendrils go clear down his abdomen and wrap up and around his shoulder to his back.

"We're going to need to get him to the hospital," the second man says, twisting around to face us. His dark, chocolate-brown eyes are empathetic as he stands up.

Rushing past me, he grabs the stretcher, dropping it beside Wade's body. Together, the two of them lift Wade up and onto the mesh of fabric, metal, and plastic.

"Ready?" Burly guy number one asks, setting his blue eyes on the empathetic one, who nods in return.

My head is a swirly cyclone of confusion and panic as they lift him up and start to remove Wade from the kitchen. But the motion of it is the kick in the ass I need.

"Wait!" I cry out. "I'm coming with you."

I follow them outside, watching them carefully maneuver the snow-covered walkways.

When we get to the back of the ambulance, they hoist Wade inside with ease, clearly used to this sort of thing. Their calm demeanor is almost unnerving as the brown-eyed man turns back to me.

"What's your relationship to this man?" he asks, holding onto the doorway and blocking my entry.

Anger courses through my body and I practically scream at him, "I'm his girlfriend."

He shakes his head, "I'm sorry. Only family can be in the ambulance with us. You'll have to meet us at the hospital."

"Are you kidding me?" I growl, getting ready to punch my way onto that ambulance if I have to.

"We'll follow you," Mom says, suddenly by my side. I hadn't even noticed her standing there. "Come on, Autumn. Let them focus on doing their job. We'll be right behind them."

I unclench my fists, swallowing hard. "*Fine*."

Spinning on my heel, I race back to the house, grabbing my purse and keys.

When I get back to the driveway, Mom is sitting in the driver's seat of Blue, with the door wide open. "Pass the keys. You're in no condition to drive."

I don't have the willpower to argue. I toss the keys and

race around to the other side. By the time I take my seat, the ambulance is starting to pull away. Mom takes off after it, staying right on its tail.

"How is this happening?" I whisper, fighting back the return of tears. "I don't know what to do."

"I don't know if there's anything you *can* do, sweetie. We need more information," Mom says, reaching out and placing her hand on my arm.

My eyes widen with her words and I reach into my front pocket. I tug out my cell phone and dial the one person I know who might be able to see what's happening —Diana Hawthorne.

The phone rings twice before she picks up. "Hey there, Autumn. Now's not a—" she pauses for a moment and sighs. "Oh god, Autumn. I'm sorry. I know this is important, but I'm right in the middle of something dire, too."

"But I need your help," I plead.

"I know you do. I'm so sorry to have to say no to this. I know it's a shitty thing to do, but you're going to need to turn to someone else."

"Someone else? Who the hell else has any sort of insights about the future?" I cry.

Mom takes the final turn to the hospital, rounding the corner a little too quickly. My insides clench as I grip the handle of the door.

"Call Dominic. He's the best one to help you," she says. "Shit, I gotta go. I'm sorry, Autumn. Call Dominic." She hangs up without even saying good-bye.

"Dammit." Without thinking, I close my fist and punch the dashboard.

Pain vibrates through my hand, but for a moment, there's clarity in the discomfort. She's right. If she's unable, or unwilling, to help me—then I need to follow her advice. I'll need to call Dominic.

The ambulance pulls into the emergency room port and Mom pulls into one of the first spots near the main entrance doors. As soon as the car is no longer in motion, I grab my purse and hop out.

Mom curses something behind me, but I don't stop to let her catch up. I need to get inside. I need to be with Wade.

I rush up to the main desk, waiting for the slight, blond woman to get off the phone. It only takes a moment, but it's long enough for me to be annoyed.

"Can I help you?" she asks, her voice calm and almost melodic.

I take a deep breath, trying to calm myself down. "Yes, I need to see my boyfriend. They just brought him in the ambulance."

The woman's fingers click against the keyboard as she turns her gaze to the monitor in front of her.

When she's taking too long to say anything, I spit, "His name is Wade Hoffman. He can't be alone—he doesn't have any family. It's just me."

"And you are?"

"His girlfriend," I say, a little too loudly.

"I'm sorry—"

"So help me, if you tell me I can't be with him because I'm not married to him, I'll punch your goddamn nose," I yell at her, practically climbing over the counter that separates us.

Mom reaches out, tugging me back. "Autumn, let the woman do her job." Her words are powerful, pulling me back from the edge of total insanity. I turn to look at her and she tips her chin and says, "*Breathe.*"

The adrenaline coursing through my veins begins to wane and I'm suddenly dizzy with exhaustion.

"No one is allowed in while they assess the patient. Relatives or not," the woman says, settling back into her seat, relief clear across her face. "If you can just take a seat while they try to figure out what's wrong, that's the best thing you can do for your boyfriend right now."

My shoulders slump as Mom grabs hold of them, turning me to face the seating area. "Thank you, dear. We appreciate it," she says to the lady behind the counter.

Mom guides me to the small alcove with uncomfortable-looking seats. The space is decorated with soft pastel colors and fake plants—clearly trying to bring as much calm to the waiting process as possible, but it falls flat.

"Sit down, Autumn," Mom says, pointing to a seat near the window.

I shake my head, walking out of her grasp as she takes her own seat. Instead, I pace in front of her, unable to shake the anxiety rolling through me.

"No, I need to call Dominic," I say, turning from her and pulling out my phone again.

Mom's eyes widen, but her mouth snaps shut as I place the phone to my ear.

Again, the phone rings a couple of times before Dominic answers. "Let me guess, Autumn's in trouble again." He chuckles softly under his breath for a moment.

My throat goes dry as I try to form the words to relay the importance in this mission. I know I suck already. I don't need to be reminded that I only call when I need help.

Dominic waits for me to respond, not even offering to search the future to see why I'm calling.

"Dominic, something has happened to Wade. Diana can't help me," I finally say.

"So you thought you'd call me," he says. "I love being a last resort. It makes me feel super special."

I roll my eyes, walking away from Mom and looking out the window on the opposite end of the waiting room. "Wade could be dying and there's something supernatural going on with him. Diana thinks you'll be the best one to help with this. That's why I'm calling you. I hate that it seems like I only call when I need something—"

"Because it's true?" Dominic interjects.

"Even if it's true, it doesn't make this any less important. Wade's mark—the one his father gave him—is infected or something. We're at the hospital now. He's in the ER and I..." I break off, fighting the tears and the quiver in my voice.

Dominic sighs. After a long pause, he says, "Okay, I'll help you figure out what's going on with loverboy. But you'll have to do me a favor first."

CHAPTER 12
LIFE, DEATH, &
METAMORPHOSIS

My mouth drops open in utter incredulousness. "You have got to be kidding me?"

I tell Dominic my boyfriend is in the *actual* emergency room, possibly dying for all I know, and the only thing he can think about is what he can get out of it? Unreal.

"Nope, that's the deal or no dice," he says, his voice like cold steel. "I'm sick of being the gopher and last resort in your little world. I have needs, too, and you can help with those *needs*."

My stomach rolls at the way he says the words and my mind automatically goes to a worst-case scenario. "What are you talking about? What needs?" I hiss, clutching the phone close and praying my mom doesn't have supersonic hearing or something.

"I know you're not big on the whole Windhaven Academy thing anymore, but I'm trying to level up. The new semester starts in a couple of weeks and I want to go into it as powerful as possible," he states matter-of-factly.

I shake my head, unable to process a thing he's asking about. I'm talking life and death and he's talking leveling up his abilities. Why am I even surprised?

"You are the most ridiculous, self-centered—" I spit.

"Cut the crap, Autumn. You're the only one who can help me with this," he says, cutting off my tirade. "It's fortuitous timing you should come to me right now."

"What in the hell do you need?" I snap, unable to hide the venom in my words.

For a long, silent moment, I hold my breath, waiting for him to explain himself.

"I need you to bring me back," he finally says, his words barely louder than a whisper.

"What?" I say, narrowing my eyes and glaring at the fake hibiscus plant in the corner.

"Look, here's the thing. I need to level up my psychic powers. As great as they seem to everyone else, they're nothing more than parlor tricks, really. But in order to trigger a metamorphosis like this... I need to face death," he says calmly.

"Level up? Metamorphosis? What kind of bullshit is this? You're not a damn butterfly, Dominic. You better not be pulling my chain. This is not the time for that if you are..." I warn.

"If I can trigger the metamorphosis, it means my abilities extend further, into the realms of the ancients. It'll help not just me, but you, too, by the sounds of it," he says. "It's not really all that complicated to understand."

I gape at the wall, walking away from where I was standing to pace again. "That's the most ridiculous reason to die. You realize that's what this is, right? Haven't you seen *Flatliners*?"

"I know what it sounds like," he retorts. "But it's not a game."

I roll my eyes. "Pretty sure it wasn't a game in the film, either..."

Dominic grunts. "Look, you have your thing and I have mine, dammit. Every time you've needed me, I've been there and helped, haven't I? Why is it so hard to believe that maybe I have something you can help with? What's the deal, Autumn? You can take, but you can't give? Or do you only help the Gilberts or that angel boyfriend of yours? Is that it?" he fires back.

I cringe at his words, but let them sink in. He's right. He may be reluctant at times, but he's always helped when we needed him. It's just that his timing sucks ass.

"Fine," I say, dropping my shoulders in defeat. "I'll help you."

What other choice do I have? I don't know if the doctors will be able to locate the source of Wade's infection fast enough and I'm not about to wait around for him to die.

"Excellent. How soon can you be here?" Dominic asks, his tone brightening.

My eyes widen and I look around the waiting room. My mom's concerned stare reaches me and I shudder. "I can't come to you. I'm in Mistwood Point. Wade's in the ER here."

"Well, how do you think you'll bring me back, then?"

"I don't know, Dominic. But I'm pretty sure we can make it work."

"Hell, no. I thought you'd need the resurrection room's energy. And maybe even *Abigail* to make this work. It's not like you're super adept at the whole resurrection thing yet.

99

I'd feel a lot better if you had some damn backup. I don't wanna die and stay dead, for crying out loud," he says, raising his voice.

"Fuck," I curse. My eyes slam shut, and I run my hand over my forehead. "Fine. *Fine*. I'm on my way. Meet me at the manor in two hours."

"No—no. You need to meet me at my house first," he says, sighing. There's something strange hidden in his tone, but before I can tell him where to shove it, he mutters, "I don't have a car right now."

My face pinches tight and I fight the urge to say that's karma for carving up my bumper before we ever met. Instead, I say through gritted teeth, "And why is that?"

Silence meets me for a moment. Just when I think I'm going to tell him where to shove it, he says, "It got repossessed, if you must know. Not everyone is as well-off as the mighty Blackwoods."

My mouth pops open and a pang of guilt stabs me in the side. As much as he can rub me the wrong way, Dominic has clearly been going through his own shit—and I had no idea. I'm such a shit friend.

"Sorry, Dom. I didn't know," I say.

"Whatever. We got our own lives. Can you come get me or not?"

"All right, your place it is. Be ready."

"I was born ready," he retorts.

"Yeah, and on that note..." I hang up the phone, rolling my eyes.

Inhaling slowly through my nose, I take a beat to consider my options one last time. Because, let's face it, is this really the best use of my time? What if shit goes sideways and I can't bring Dominic back? What if he comes back...*wrong*? It's not like things were super-stellar with Cat when I brought her back. Part of her soul split off and became a Fetch, for godsake.

But on the other side, I don't know how I'll find the information I need to help Wade if I don't. This is clearly magical or supernatural in nature. And if Diana can't help me, Dominic really is my next-best option.

Plus, if I leave now, there's a chance I can get all the information I need in just a few hours. It's likely Wade will be in there for a while anyway and time is of the essence. I can't just sit here in this hospital waiting for someone to help him or...

Shuddering away the thought, I rush over to my mom.

The place between her eyebrows scrunches as I approach. "Where are you going?"

"The manor. I have someone who can help me. Well, help Wade... But I need to be there in person," I say, trying to keep my tone light.

"Now's not a good time, Autumn. You really shouldn't drive when you're so upset. It's not safe," she says, her tone as cold as ice.

At least she hasn't used her "mom voice" yet.

"I know. It's not ideal. Trust me, if there was any other way, I'd be doing it," I say.

She stands up, shaking her head. "No, I should drive. You really shouldn't be alone right now."

My eyes widen at the prospect and I shake my head. "No, Mom. It's fine—I'm fine. I need to take care of this on my own."

"What about the Moirai? If they come for you while you're separated—"

"Mom, this is Wade. It's a risk I have to take."

Her eyes narrow. "You're pregnant, Autumn. It's not just your life you're putting in jeopardy."

Again, I flinch at her words. She's totally right, but I'm backed into a damn corner and I have to take control of *something*.

"I won't be alone for long. When I get to Windhaven, I'm picking up Dominic. He's going to help me figure out what's happening to Wade," I say, trying to sound reasonable.

"Dominic Crane?" she says, surprise flashing through her features.

I nod.

"He never could stay away from you," she mutters, shaking her head. She watches me closely, but surprisingly, tips her head. "Go. I'll stay and keep you posted if anything new happens."

"Are you sure you want to stay? It might be a while and you don't have a car here," I say.

"I know just about every person in this town. If I need to, I can hitch a ride home. Now, go. But please, for the love of all that's holy—*be careful*." She reaches into her pocket, relinquishing the keys to Blue.

"Thanks, Mom," I whisper, bending forward and kissing her on the cheek, taking the keys from her.

She wraps her arms around me, clutching me tightly for a long moment. When she lets go, I inhale deeply, stealing some courage in the air between us. Then, I straighten my shoulders and head for the door. I don't even look back at the unhelpful woman behind the counter or the place where the ambulance vanished into the building.

Instead, I go straight for Blue and get inside. The

hysteria that consumed me before has faded into a determination like I've never felt before.

I will find a way to save Wade. If it means going to Windhaven and helping Dominic, so be it.

The only saving grace in all of this is that I haven't seen any red threads surrounding Wade or these events. Maybe it means this has nothing to do with the Moirai. Maybe it's something else entirely—something that can be fixed, if we just know where to look.

I hold onto that thought as I pull out of the parking lot and put my foot to the gas. It should take me two hours to get to Windhaven from here, but I have every intention of making it there in an hour or less.

My thoughts span from doing everything I can to help Wade as quickly as possible, to organizing the logistics of how to flatline Dominic and bring him back. It's the most ludicrous balancing act I've ever been put in charge of and the irony isn't lost on me at all.

I mean, what if all of this is really pulling me away from Wade when I should be there with him? He's no longer an Angel of Death—so that means if he dies, he's... gone. No coming back and being born again as something else. At this point, even that would be better than this.

Suddenly, a horrible idea surfaces and I bite back my terror. Everything is stemming from his mark. The mark put there by his dad. What if he decided it was time to wipe the slate clean and kill Wade off? Would he do something like that knowing he'd be dead and gone?

Unless, of course, I was there to resurrect him. But as Dominic so aptly pointed out, I'm not necessarily the expert on it yet. I could end up making everything worse.

There's also nothing to say that any of this will work

with Dominic, either. But I guess I'm more okay with him being the guinea pig over Wade, as awful as that sounds.

I just hope that when I bring Dominic back, he's still got his faculties and is able to do what I need him to. I mean, what if we mess with this bizarre idea of trying to trigger a metamorphosis to make him more powerful, and it backfires?

CHAPTER 13
PITY PARTY & NEGOTIATIONS

The farther I get from Wade, the more my insides scream to turn back around. Instead, I push the panic aside, letting it fuel my foot as I press it to the pedal and drive as fast as I can to Windhaven.

When I reach Dominic's house, I practically drift into his driveway, coming to a burnt halt. I honk the horn to signal I'm here, but when he doesn't exit the building fast enough, I hop out of my vehicle and stomp up the steps to his front door.

As I lift my fist to pound on the door, it flies open. "That was fast," Dominic says, bewilderment splattered across his face.

"I told you to be ready," I grumble. "Let's go." I twist around, shoving both of my hands in the direction of Blue.

"Hang on," Dominic says. "I have to do something quick."

I release an exasperated sigh. "I practically broke the speed barrier to get here and now you wanna screw around?"

He shoots me an irritated glance but walks back inside anyway.

Clenching my fists, I scream internally, but follow him. Dusk has fallen and the house is dimly lit with only a couple of small lamps here and there. Dominic walks past the staircase on the right and continues his way down a hallway to what looks like a living room that's been converted into a bedroom. There are stacks of books, magazines, and knickknacks smattered all over the room. There's also a small dresser with drawers half open and clothing dangling out of each. The floor is a mess of plates, cups, and liquor bottles.

I step forward tentatively, eyeing the room with a new sense of suspicion. There's a thick stench of vomit. What's going on here?

Dominic holds his hand up as he walks over to the sofa and crouches down beside it. "Mom, I'm going to be out for a bit."

A thin, white hand rises from behind the puffy flower-covered fabric of the sofa.

"Wheresyagoin?" Her response is slurred into a single word and it's clear she's the one who's been drinking.

"Just over to Blackwood Manor for a little bit." He shifts his gaze to me and swallows hard. "I won't be gone long."

"Whateryadoin o'er there?" she asks, clutching at his shoulder.

He pats her hand, removing its viselike grip and resting it with her. "I just need to help Autumn with something quick. I'll be back before you know it," he says, standing up and kissing her forehead. "Love you, Mom."

She grumbles something that sounds like, "Yeah, you, too."

He lingers there for a second longer, his face a mix of emotions. With a sharp nod, he turns on his heel and heads back over to where I stand gaping at him. I close my mouth, but his mortified expression tells me he's not happy I followed him in.

"You coming or what?" he spits as he stalks past me.

Turning to walk out with him, I shoot one last glance over my shoulder at his mother. The last time I was there, I hadn't noticed her. Then again, I can't say we ventured this far into the house, either.

A pang of sympathy for Dominic stabs me in the gut. How long has he been dealing with this?

By the time I exit the front door, Dominic is already in the passenger seat and buckling himself in. I walk around my SUV with much less gusto than when I left it.

As I get into the driver's seat and put Blue into drive, his eyes stare straight ahead of him.

"So, that was your mom, huh?" I say, finally breaking the silence.

"Yup," he says, popping the P as a final punctuation.

I inhale sharply through my nose and exhale slowly, unsure what to say that would make things any easier for him.

"Don't get your panties in a twist. This is nothing new," he says, giving me the side eye. When I look at him, surprised, he adds, "Your thoughts are pretty damn loud."

"Oh," I mutter. "Right."

We sit in tense silence as I drive toward my house.

"She wasn't always like this," he mutters, shaking his head. "But when Dad left her a couple of years ago..." His words dwindle out and he turns to look out the passenger-side window.

I didn't know any of this about him and I can't help but feel absolutely terrible about that fact.

"Dominic," I begin.

"If you're gonna say you're sorry for me, so help me, woman, I'll throw myself out of this moving vehicle," he mutters, still not removing his eyes from the passing scenery.

"Is this why you want to level up so bad?" I ask, clutching the steering wheel tighter.

He shrugs. "I can't live my life for Mom. Hell, she's not even willing to live it for herself."

"Then why?"

"What else do I have? You've seen the state of my house. We're one of the founding families here in Windhaven and we're falling apart. Dead broke. The house is in shambles. Mom's a drunk. Dad left... We're probably going to be homeless soon. Hell, they took my fucking car," he says, anger building in his tone.

Something in his pity party sparks the anger inside myself and I shake my head. "You've gotta be kidding me. As if your life is so bad. Sure, some shit sucks—but at least no one is actively dying. You're not being stalked by the Moirai for something you didn't even do. And if you don't find a way to break the curse, your entire family tree is going to be *wiped out*."

Dominic's blue eyes widen and he turns to face me. "What?"

"Yeah, welcome to my life right now, Dom. I'm sorry, I'm a shitty friend. I get that. But your life isn't as bad as you think it is. Does some of it suck? No question. But you still have a full life ahead of you. You can *be* anyone you want. Hell, be *with* anyone you want. I can't even be afforded that luxury without the Angel of Death screwing things over," I say, snorting to myself.

It feels good to voice my frustrations, even if they're not actually meant for Dominic.

His eyebrows flick upward and he snickers. "Shit, we're both a pair, aren't we?"

"Yeah," I mutter, turning down my driveway and hitting the gas.

In less than a minute, I traverse the rest of the drive and skid to a stop in the front loop of the house. I don't say a word as I get out of the car and make my way to the front door.

Dominic follows a step or two behind me. I fling my keys on the entryway table and keep going until I reach my bedroom. As I step inside, I reach over, flipping the lights on. The room bursts with illumination as the lamps turn on in unison.

"I'd hate to be the one paying your electric bill," Dominic mutters.

Allowing my anger to continue fueling me, I ignore his comment as I turn around and place my hands on my hips. "All right, I need you to help me figure out what's happening with Wade. Then, as promised, I'll help you *level up*."

The words come out colder than I intended, and he cringes.

"No, we have to do the flatline first," Dominic insists. "Before you got here, I tried to put some feelers out there, but was getting blocked. It's like there are some magical wards up around him. Who knows, maybe it's an angel thing. If I level up, I'll have a better chance of under-standing what's what."

I narrow my gaze and shake my head, almost a hundred percent sure he's giving me a line of crap. Especially since Wade's no longer on the list to become an angel.

"No dice," I say. "What if you flatline and I can't bring you back? Did you even think of that?"

"Why do you think I told my mom I loved her," he fires back, jutting out his chin.

My mouth falls open as I pull up short. "Oh, I didn't mean..." I say, backpedaling. I blink away my shock and drop my gaze to the floor. I glance up in time to see him roll his eyes and it sets me off again. My jaw hardens and nostrils flare. "Well, even if everything goes according to plan—*and it should*—I'll still be a mess if I'm worrying about Wade the whole time. I'll be no good to you. I still say we do this my way."

Dominic makes a face, clearly fighting with himself. "Dammit, woman. Fine. Sit your ass down. Let's see what we can dredge up on your boyfriend. But if I get nothing, we're switching gears. Get it?"

"Fine," I spit, plopping down right where I stand like a defiant child.

Dominic saunters over, taking a seat in the middle of the floor with me.

We sit cross-legged opposite each other, and he holds his hands out. I look down at them as if he's lost his mind.

He glares at me. "Get over yourself. We need to create a circle so I can get a better read on him."

Reluctantly, I reach out, placing my hands in his.

"All right, I need you to focus on your connection to Loverboy. Think about what's happening, what you know, what you don't know. All of it," Dominic says, sitting up straighter and closing his eyes.

His face settles into a blank slate, clearing off any animosity or emotions from our exchange.

"Focus," he whispers, tilting his head slightly.

My eyes flicker shut, and I do as I'm asked. I think about Wade...our connection, his birthright, the mark of expulsion, the infection as it took him over, the Moirai—all of it.

The events flicker behind my eyelids and I can tell the information is coming in strong for Dominic, too. He holds still, barely breathing as he consumes the information coming at him.

After a few moments, he says, "The mark—what did you think it was?"

"His father said it was the mark of expulsion. He's no longer going to be an angel," I whisper, opening my eyes.

Dominic's eyes remain shut and his head is tilted, like he's listening to something in the air.

"Hmmm," he says, his forehead wrinkling in concentration.

"What? What do you see? What can we do?" I ask, gripping his hands tighter.

"There's so much haze around it. It's like it's all wrapped up in a magical snowball. The Moirai are a part of this. The mark..." he says, shaking his head. "There's something off about the mark."

"No shit. It's infecting him. Whatever it is, it's spread all over his torso. He said"—my voice cracks as I remember his last words—"he said he could smell burnt flesh and hair."

"I don't get it. Every time I try to understand this

mark, it's like it starts to get clear, then moves out of focus," he says, shaking his head.

"What do you think that means?"

"I'm not..." he gapes at me, yanking his hands back. "Holy shit—you're pregnant?"

"I don't know that it's any of your business," I say, blinking hard at him.

Dominic scrambles to his feet. "Like hell. You wanted to know what's happening—what's coming. How am I supposed to be effective when I don't have all the information?"

"You're psychic. I figured you'd find the information that was relevant. It's not like I was trying to hide anything. I just found out. He doesn't even know. And besides, I'm not asking about being pregnant," I say, blinking back tears. "I'm trying to *save Wade*."

"Well, then things just got a helluva lot more complicated for you," he snickers under his breath.

I gape at him, waiting for him to explain himself.

After a moment, he shakes his head and meets my gaze. "Look, I need more intel—the kind I can get when I level up. But I can tell you the Moirai aren't just searching for a way to take you and Wade down. They're coming for your baby, too."

My heart races as I push myself to a stand. It's not like I didn't know this—the curse has damned us all. But it's something entirely different to hear that it's set in motion.

If they plan on taking out our child, the easiest way to do that would be to end his or her life before the baby has a chance of being born.

That means time's almost up and I'm running out of options.

CHAPTER 14

AN INSANE GAMBLE

The room spins, and I walk over to the bed and take a seat.

For some reason I thought I'd have more time. If nothing else, the duration of the pregnancy, before shit hit the fan. But if they're coming for all of us, all bets are off.

"When are they coming, Dominic? Has it started already? Is that what this is? They're attacking Wade?" I ask, tears blurring my vision.

Dom shakes his head. "I don't know. Like I said, the whole situation around him is weird—there's so much interference."

"Then make it clearer," I spit at him.

"I can't," he says, throwing his hands in the air. "I'm not omnipotent, for fucksake. I've been trying to tell you, my abilities have *limits*."

I narrow my gaze. "So, basically, you're withholding information until you get what you want?"

"What?" he sputters, making a face. "No. That's not what this is."

"Maybe this was a mistake," I say, dropping my gaze to the floor. The room still feels like it's rotating and my stomach is precariously on the verge of pushing the contents back up.

I swallow hard, trying to ignore the pressure.

Dominic opens his mouth to say something, but my phone rings, cutting off whatever he planned on spouting out. I tug my phone from my pocket, and flip it over. It's my mom.

For a second, my heart stops beating.

"Hey, Mom. Is Wade—" I sputter, trying not to panic.

"He's stable for now and they've moved him from the ER to the ICU. Unfortunately, that's as much as they can tell me at the moment, sweetie. How are you doing there? Did you make it okay?" she says, trying to keep her voice calm and even.

I shift my gaze to Dominic and nod. "Yeah, I made it okay. I'm with Dom now, but I'll be back soon."

"Okay, I'll call if I hear anything else. Text when you're on your way back, okay?" she says.

"Yeah, okay," I say.

"Love you, Autumn."

"Love you, too, Mom," I say, hanging up the phone.

Again, my gaze flits to Dominic. Things are just as ominous for me now as they were when he said the same thing to his mother.

He takes a deep breath, cramming his hands into his pockets. "Look, Autumn, I know this is the last thing you want to do right now, but it's really important to me. And if all goes according to plan, me leveling up might be the one thing you need in order to protect yourself from this curse. Obviously, your dad's research didn't save him. This isn't just about Wade anymore."

I stand up. "Don't you think I know that?"

"Well, then, what the hell are you waiting for?" he spits back.

I blink back angry tears and I ask myself the same question. Then, it finally dawns on me. It has nothing to do with helping him with this, or even the timing so much.

"I've been surrounded by death from the moment I came back to Windhaven. I just lost my dad, my boyfriend's in the ER, and as you said, time is running out for everyone. Myself and my baby included," I say softly, my hands instinctively lowering to my abdomen. "Why would I want to *intentionally* kill a friend, just to test whether or not I can bring him back? Right now, it seems like an insane gamble."

Dominic's blue eyes widen and for a moment, he doesn't say anything.

I pinch the bridge of my nose. "Look, I know you think I only reach out to you when I need something, and maybe there's some truth in that. But you're one of my good friends, Dominic. I don't have many of those and I don't want to lose you, too," I whisper.

His chin juts out, rolling it from side to side as he fights the emotion welling in his eyes. "Yeah, well...the feeling is mutual," he says, his voice cracking. "There's just one difference."

"What's that?" I say, looking at him from under my eyebrows.

"I don't think it's a *completely* insane gamble." His lips twitch slightly.

I roll my eyes, dropping my gaze to the phone still clutched in my hand. Wade's stable, but for how long? Dominic's right, we need more answers and if getting him to level up his abilities could help us with this, maybe it really is the answer we've been looking for.

"All right, what do we do next? How do we make this work?" I say, biting down on my lip to keep it from quivering.

Ending *anything* isn't my specialty—and deliberately ending a friend's life is so far out of my comfort zone, I can't even fathom it.

"From what I've been able to gather, we just need to stop my heart from beating. Then, you bring me back," he says, far more calmly than I would, if roles were reversed.

"You make it sound like you're just going to the grocery store or something," I mutter, raking my fingertips over my face.

"Well, it's the way it works," he says, shrugging. "You were going to be a forensic scientist in a past life, right? Surely you have to know a thing or two about how to manage this?"

I glare at him. "I wanted to understand how people died so I could solve their deaths and bring peace to the people who loved them. Not use my abilities as a way to make them die. I'm not a sociopath."

"Well, it only needs to be for a few seconds," he says, trying to sound reasonable. "Don't you—I don't know, doesn't your grimoire have information on how to make something like this happen?"

I make a face and snicker. "I highly doubt that."

Dominic paces back and forth for a moment, rubbing his hand across his mouth. "All right, I just need to go into cardiac arrest, right? Damn, where's Cat when you need her?"

"Cat? What's she got to do with this?" I snort.

"Well, she can manipulate fire and electricity. She coulda shocked the hell out of me." A dry laugh leaves his lips.

"Since when can she manipulate electricity?" I ask, surprised.

Dominic stares back at me incredulously. "You really *do* suck at checking in with friends."

I sigh, starting to get irritated again. "Come on. Let's go to the Resurrection Chamber and I'll summon Abigail. Maybe she'll know something I don't."

I stalk past him and over to the small door leading to the basement. After my father's Lemure destroyed half of the house, I didn't have the heart to redesign the door into anything more than what it was. It felt sacrilegious somehow. So, while it's still half the size of a normal door, the new stairs are far more stable. They're now crafted in stone slabs rather than rickety wooden planks.

When we reach the sandy floor, Dominic stops, taking a good look around. He doesn't say anything—he doesn't have to. The mess took weeks to clean up, but thankfully, the majority of the stones from the walls were able to be repaired and put back. In fact, if you didn't know about the destruction, nothing about the space looks out of the ordinary.

"Abigail," I call out, knowing that she'll come to me without question now. After my father's soul was laid to rest, the extra energy and effort she had to expel trying to keep him under control is no longer necessary. She now comes and goes as easily as any of us, which is both a relief and unnerving.

Within seconds, she's by my side, giving Dominic a curious, arched eyebrow. Then she turns her curiosity to me. "What is it, child?"

"Abigail, we need your help. Do you know..." I drop my gaze, unsure how this will sound to her. "Do you now how to instigate a death for the sake of being brought back?"

Her lips press into a thin line. "Is this the conception of the Crane boy?"

Dominic narrows his gaze. "What is she saying? I can feel her presence, but she's blocking me out."

I glance his direction. "I don't think she's impressed with your plan."

He shrugs, as if he expected as much.

"Dominic thinks he might be able to help our family. But he feels the only way to do that is by leveling up his powers," I say, choosing my words carefully. If Abigail knows this could be to the benefit of our lineage, she'll be more inclined to help.

Stepping away from me, she wrings her hands and shakes her head. "This is a most dreadful idea. The eternal law of self-preservation may prevent any of this—"

"But is he right? Is it possible for him to increase his powers this way?" I ask, suddenly intensely curious.

If he can, does that explain Cat's new ability to manipulate electricity as well as fire?

Abigail steels herself for a moment, then turns back to me. "It is risky, to be certain. He must lift the veil, separating himself from the earthly and astral planes. He must voyage to the other side, connecting with the source of his powers, before being summoned back. Should any of these pieces go wrong..."

"But it's possible," I say, latching onto the one thing that gives me a glimmer of hope.

Her lips press tightly, but she nods.

Dominic steps forward, his eyes sweeping around the stone chamber. "Abigail, I know this probably sounds insane to you, but it's important. *Trust me.*"

His final words resonate with such strong sentiment, I suck in a breath. He's desperate to do this, but he truly believes this is the only way. Whether it's for himself, or for the sake of my family, I don't know. But if the results are the same, I don't care.

Abigail's forehead creases, but she drops her chin and whispers. "There is a way for a necromancer to help lift the veil for another."

"*Good*—that's good. Right?" I say.

"What is it?" Dominic asks.

I hold up an index finger to have him wait a moment.

"The magic is but a remnant; however, I am quite certain it would do as you ask," she says.

"Fine," I say, shaking my head. "What do we need to do?"

Apprehension and anxiety roll themselves into one big ball in my stomach, and my imagination rolls through different ways I might have to employ to kill Dominic. I shudder them away.

"As necromancers, our natural state is to tread lightly between the world of the living and that of the dead. The veil is not an obstacle for us the way it is for most. If a soul is coaxed from a body with the correct potion, it will simulate death, and we may be able to guide it across from this side. However, should his soul linger there for too long..." Her voice lowers in a warning.

"He won't be able to return," I finish for her.

She nods.

Dominic's eyes widen as he watches me.

Turning to him I say, "Abigail thinks it can be done. But it'll take time. We need to create a potion, I guess. Something that will force your soul from your body."

Dominic's face pulls in tight and he reaches into his jeans pocket. "You've gotta understand, I've felt this coming for a while. Okay? But today, I went into a trance trying to find my way to make this work and when I came to, I had written some ingredients on a piece of paper," he says, grinning sheepishly. "I wasn't sure what it was, but I figured I'd use it as my last resort if you didn't help. Guess that wasn't why I was called to create it."

He reaches his hand out, dropping a small vial into my palm. I pick it up, spinning it between my fingertips. The liquid glows with a strange purple, glittery energy. Holding it out to Abigail, I ask, "Does this look like the potion we need? Or is this something else?"

Abigail steps forward, peering into the depths of it. After a moment, she nods. "It appears to be so. Does the Crane boy remember its contents?"

"She wants to know what's in it," I say, relaying the message.

Dom shrugs. "Not much, really. Lavender, lemon mixed with holy water, and powdered belladonna root. Oh, and a drop of my blood, for some reason."

Abigail watches him closely. "What of its creation? Was it warmed with the Necrosis Flame?"

"Did you use the Necrosis Flame to stew the ingredients?" I ask, sighing heavily.

"What the hell is the Necrosis Flame? That sounds like it should be your area of expertise, not mine," he sputters.

Immediately, any hopes that we might have an easy way out of this are dashed. I turn back to Abigail, who says, "All is not lost. The Crane boy is right; this is more our area of expertise."

"Okay?" I say, enclosing the vial in my palm.

"The Necrosis Flame can be summoned by a necromancer for various reasons. Some are intentional, while others are not. In a necromancer, it often springs forth as visual indicator or warning system that someone's life force is in a state of active disturbance. But when used intentionally, it produces an ethereal flame capable of brewing the Feign Death Potion," she says, tipping her chin high as she clasps her hands behind her back.

"The Feign Death Potion?" I say, practically laughing at the name.

"Is that what this is?" Dominic asks.

I nod. "Almost."

"Because I am no longer of the living, I cannot spring forth this flame, but you can, my dear. You simply need to concentrate on it to make it happen," Abigail says, beginning to pace.

"Concentrate? Like with the astral projection? Or—?"

"Have you never felt a time when the Necrosis Flame was triggered unintentionally?" she asks.

Shaking my head, I snicker. "Not that I can think of."

But suddenly, my wry laughter is cut short as I think of all those times with Colton.

"What is it?" Abigail asks, narrowing her gaze.

Inhaling a deep breath, I tilt my head, shifting through all of the times the flames erupted with Colton. "I think maybe I have, actually."

"Good, then you know its vibration. I want you to close your eyes and call upon it."

Doing as I'm told, I close my eyes, thinking about Colton and the flames. I have no idea the flames were a warning about his life force—and it suddenly has me worrying that he might not be as immortal as everyone thinks he is.

However, when I open my eyes, I look down to find my hand consumed by the same orange and blue flames. And though it's fully engulfed by it, my hand is completely unscathed. However, inside my palm, the contents of the vial begin to boil.

I stare down at the bubbling liquid until, abruptly, the flames go out.

"I believe we can now proceed," she says, her face stoic. "But do so *cautiously*."

Nodding to her, I turn to Dominic and hold the vial back out to him.

"I have no idea what just happened. You know that, right?" he mutters, accepting the small glass object.

"That's okay. All you need to know is we're ready to go now," I say.

"He will wish to be lying down before drinking the potion. It takes but seconds to work," Abigail says, continuing to pace around the room like a caged animal.

"Dominic, lie down on the floor, then drink the potion," I say, pointing to the middle of the room.

Without another thought, he tips his chin in acknowledgement, then moves to sit down. Uncorking the top, he doesn't even verify the timing or go over the plan again. He just slams the contents and lets the empty vial clatter across the ground.

He opens his mouth, probably to say something, but his eyes immediately roll to the back of his head. I dash over, reaching him just in time to ease his torso to the ground.

"Now, you must focus on summoning his soul from his body. See in your mind's eye walking with him through the veil from this world to the next, but do not allow yourself to be pulled with him. You must stay on this side in order to awaken him," Abigail says, her furrowed eyebrows scrunched in thought.

"Nothing to it," I whisper to myself, unsure any of this is a good idea at all. But at least it's in motion and I have no choice but to make this work.

Still kneeling beside him, I close my eyes and focus on calling Dominic's soul from the confines of his body. Behind my eyelids a bright, blue orb forms.

"Good. Very good," Abigail mutters her approval. There's a strange admiration in her tone and I know this must be something she wishes she could do for herself.

I settle into the energy, allowing it to fill up my perception. It's not all that unlike astral-projecting, but it feels different. Denser somehow. It doesn't take long to latch onto Dominic's energy, but rather than forming as a person, I continue to see the blue orb within my mind's eye. A silver string also extends from the orb, making its way out of the darkness. Suddenly, as if the orb knows what it needs to do, it sails out and away from me. It vanishes through time and space, pulled somehow into what seems like a black hole. However, the silver string remains, floating like chemtrails in the air.

When I open my eyes, I realize it's attached to his abdomen.

"The rest is now up to him," Abigail says. "He had but moments, so be ready."

I nod, exhaling a tense breath.

While astral-projecting is similar, walking to the edge of the veil was something else. There was a darkness beyond—an energy that consumed all light, if you weren't careful. And I'm not sure whether or not sending Dominic into that was a wise choice.

"It is time," Abigail says. "Summon the boy back."

Nodding to her, I close my eyes, and take a deep breath. Unlike when I tried to bring Cat back, there's a deep, powerful connection—like a direct line that binds us together. I can already tell that I don't need some of the other ingredients, like the blood—or even the invocation. His soul, the bright blue orb, is right before me. All I need to do is encourage him to return to his vessel.

Like a conductor, I raise my arms in front of me, trying to guide it back to where it belongs.

"That's it," Abigail says, her voice lifting in tone. "Continue with the intention."

Exhaling any nervous energy, I focus on the orb, directing it lower. When it reaches Dominic's body, it hovers there. Rather than sinking back into his body, the energy is more like two magnets with opposing forces trying to connect.

"Something is not right," I say, narrowing my gaze and trying harder.

"He is choosing to stay separated," Abigail says, her eyes distant.

"What?" I spit. "Why would he do that?"

Abigail shakes her head. "Of that, I do not know."

"Goddammit, Dominic," I cry out, dropping to my knees and shaking his body. "Get your ass back to me. You promised you'd help me."

A new kind of panic flashes through me and I rake my fingers through my hair.

What is he doing? This is the last thing I need right now and he *knows* that.

So, why the hell won't he come back?

CHAPTER 15
THE OTHER SIDE

My blood boils, and I imagine the various ways I'm going to kick Dominic's ass when I finally get him back.

"Come back. Right now," I cry out, clutching at his shoulders and shaking his torso. The silver string remains, but with each passing moment, it seems to fade.

His body is limp and the edges of his lips are taking on a faint bluish tint.

I shake my head in disbelief. "Oh, no you don't..."

Closing my eyes, I try to tap into universal energies and the deeper parts of my gifts—parts I didn't know existed, as I try to summon him back. Without thinking about the words, they spring to my lips. "Dominic Crane— wandering soul, I summon you back from the realm of the dead. Return, fragments of soul and self, from that of the spirit realm, to re-inhabit the body."

I open my eyes and for a brief moment, the blue orb of light grows brighter, but it doesn't get any closer to his body.

"Fuck," I spit, slamming the side of my fist into the dirt. "What am I doing wrong?"

"This is of no one's doing but his own. The boy is refusing to come back," Abigail whispers feverishly beside my ear.

"How do I get him back?" I say through gritted teeth.

Abigail's lips press tight and she shakes her head.

"Don't you dare tell me there's no way," I say, reeling on her. "There *has* to be a way. I'll drag him back kicking and screaming if I have to."

Her eyebrows tug in and her nostrils flare as if the thought of it is distasteful. However, she whispers, "If you are to stand any chance, it would come at great risk."

I'm suddenly on my feet. "How do I do it?" I demand.

Abigail's expression is grim as she says, "Your *soul* must leave your body to follow after him."

"So, how is that any different from what I've been doing? Astral projection and all that. Hell, what I just did —" I start.

"It is not the same. You leave this plane of existence entirely to enter the realm of the dead. There's only one way to do that," she says, frowning.

My fingers curl into fists as I glare at her. "Would you spit it out already? We're running out of time."

"It's not your consciousness that travels with this. It's your *soul*. Should you go there, you risk not coming back," she says, setting her jaw. "It takes a strong will to return to the living without an anchor on this side."

"So, be my anchor," I say, as if the answer to the question was completely obvious.

She shakes her head. "I cannot. I'm not of this plane. I'm somewhere between."

"Great, just...great," I say, walking away from her and nodding to myself. "Well, looks like I have no other choice. It's now or never."

"Autumn," she says, the warning lingering in my name.

I wave a hand, dismissing her worry. "Hey, I've done it once, right? Why not go two for two?"

She inhales sharply. "This is not a game, child."

"Then I guess I better get to *work*." Determination settles around me and I know she feels it. "Are you going to help me get this started?"

Abigail paces for a moment, wringing her hands. If she could be any more pale, I would swear she had lost a little more color. But finally, she tips her head. "I will do what I can. But the rest will be unto you."

"Deal," I say, nodding.

She returns the gesture, setting her concerned gaze on me. "Do you remember how it felt to be at the veil's edge?"

"Yes," I whisper.

"Good," she tips her chin. "Go there again. When you arrive, cross the threshold. But brace yourself. That will be the moment when your soul will disentangle itself."

"What should I expect?" I ask, raising an eyebrow.

She shakes her head. "Of that I do not know." Her arms sweep out, suggesting to herself.

"Oh, right."

"You should contact someone. A living relative or—"

"No, absolutely not. There's no time," I say, cutting her off. "So, here goes nothing."

For some reason, I'm compelled to lie down, so I do so. Resting next to Dominic, I reach out, grabbing hold of his hand, hoping it will act as a divining rod of sorts once I cross into the realm of the dead.

Anxiety and fears erupt in the middle of my solar plexus, but I push them down, refusing to give them space in my head. If I do, I know I'll change my mind and everything will be lost.

Closing my eyes, I allow my body to relax until it feels as though it's sinking into the dirt beneath me. Suddenly, I'm traveling beyond the confines of the resurrection chamber—whirling through the dense fog of the aether.

I follow the trail of Dominic's silver string to the point where it disappears into nothingness. For a moment, I wait, staring into the utter blackness beyond. This is the mystery of the ages—scholars and philosophers the world over have wanted to know what's on the other side, and here I am, about to go through with no desire to share any of it with the world.

I just want my friend back.

Settling into my conviction, I push myself beyond the edge of the known and into the darkness. Everything about who I am and why I'm here is ripped from me as I plummet through the gloom. Who I am, all that I was, feels like it's compressed and the pressure of it is beyond excruciating.

Almost as if my body was sucked down a drain and spat back out, I find myself somewhere else entirely. At first, nothing makes sense. There's screaming coming from somewhere—and everywhere. One moment I'm in a dark tunnel, blood dripping from the walls. The next moment, I'm in the middle of a large field full of tiny blue flowers.

Then I'm back within a dark cavern space and gruesome figures cling to the walls, fighting with restraints only they can see.

Everything is dizzying and I can't seem to find my bearings in this place.

I stumble backward as a man with half a face crawls out of the darkness. His bony, half-decomposed hand reaches out for me, clutching at my leg. I hop back, struggling to get out of his reach, only to realize he's no longer there.

Groping at my chest, I take a deep breath, but it's solely out of habit—because somewhere in the back of my perception, I realize I'm no longer in my body. I'm alive, but...not.

What does that make me?

The thought is a curious one, and I contemplate it for a moment, trying to remember what it was that brought me to this place.

Music plays somewhere, and I'm suddenly walking down a well-lit, open hallway toward it. It calls me at such a deep level, and the concept of it widens until it's the only thing in the entire universe.

Drawn to it at such a deep level, I can't imagine being anywhere where this music doesn't exist. The simple thought of that makes my soul ache.

Soul.

It's such a simple thought—a simple word, but it sparks something inside me and I look around. A faint silver string captures my attention and I reach for it. It vibrates softly in my hand and information is passed through it straight into my consciousness.

I'm meant to follow it.

Curiosity burns inside my awareness and with the string resting gently across my fingertips, I move forward, allowing it to guide me. The dark and gruesome images subside, giving way to a large wooded area. The trees are enormous and lush, some draping their branches across the ground as they sway lightly in the breeze.

The trees open up, revealing a small pond. Steam rises from it, catching the sun's rays in its search for the sky. Far out on the other side, swans gracefully settle into the water, making me smile.

I edge closer, wanting to see them more clearly. As I do, an old dock extends outward like a boardwalk to infinity. Without thought, I step onto, walking out as far as I dare.

When I reach the end, I take a seat, letting my legs dangle off the edge. Though I don't remember taking off my shoes, my feet are bare and I dip my toes into the water. Oddly enough, I don't feel a thing.

I stare at my feet, curious about the lack of sensation. However, my gaze moves from my feet, to the reflection in the water beyond. My red hair is wild with the wind and sun, but my face is far too young. For some reason, I can't remember what I'm meant to look like, but I'm certain it wasn't this.

I'm older. Right?

Twisting around on the dock, I scramble to my feet. Something isn't right about all of this.

I'm lost...

Something glitters in the sunlight, demanding my scrutiny. I race down the dock, listening to the way my feet press upon the boards, making the most haunting music. When I reach the spot that caught my eye, I pick it up, and once again, it's the silver string.

Had I dropped it?

Determined not to lose my focus again, I hold the

string firmly between my fingers and palm, using it like a guide rope to my destination.

The string leads me to an area on the other edge of the pond and while I can see the string ends, I can't fathom how it does so. It's as though it vanishes into nothingness.

Stepping up to the end, I run my hand along the string to the point it no longer exists. Surprisingly, my hand pushes straight through, vanishing along with the string.

Confused, I pull my hand back and stare at it. While it seems whole and complete, there's something in the back of my mind that tells me this isn't how it's supposed to be.

All of a sudden, a remarkable resolve washes over me and I pick up the string again. With it clutched in my hand, I close my eyes, walking forward into the space where the string vanished.

When I open my eyes, I'm no longer outside by a pond, but instead, in an enormous garage.

The space is sparsely decorated with metal shelving and storage units. Light streams in the windows, illuminating the pain in cars before me. Suddenly aware of them, I realize the space is full of vehicles of all makes and models. They're all lined up, going down as far as the eye can see.

With the string still clutched in my hand, I follow it around to the front of the nearest vehicle. The blues and purples in the paint sparkle like a fireworks display and I bend in, mesmerized. Then, to the right, movement catches my eye, making me jump.

I nearly drop the string, but instead, clutching it tight, I race to the front of the car to get a better view. The string tugs back, pulling me forward and I practically stumble as I make my way to the front of the cars.

Gripping it tighter, I'm startled as I realize the string is attached to a body.

And not just *any* body, either.

Dominic leans back, resting his elbows on the hood of a bright red sports car. "We'll it's about damn time."

CHAPTER 16
THEM'S THE RULES

My thoughts sputter as I try to pull them into a cohesive unit. Nothing makes sense at first, but Dominic doesn't give me long to question it. He hops off the car and walks over to me like a man on a mission.

"I was beginning to think I overestimated your abilities," he says, smirking at me.

I shake my head, trying to clear the confusion. "I don't understand."

"Look, we don't have a whole helluva lot of time here, so let me get straight to the point. You have a lot of work to do and it means getting serious now."

He steps forward, tapping my forehead with the tip of his middle finger.

Suddenly, everything that's brought us to this moment comes flooding back to me with an intense clarity that makes me double over.

I blink back my surprise at how easily I was confused and led astray in this realm.

"It's not just you," Dominic says, clearly reading my thoughts. "This place is meant to break you down to your simplest form. Heaven, hell. It's all here."

"What?" I say, narrowing my gaze.

"You must have felt it—the pull through all the good and the bad. But ultimately, you end up one place or another. Your heaven or your hell, based off your soul's experiences. Mine is clearly taking form as—this," he says, widening his arms and twirling around. "Gotta admit, it's not a bad place to be."

"You can't stay here," I say, suddenly filled with anger. "Why wouldn't you come back? You promised to help me."

"And I am," he says, cocking his head to the side. "We needed a safe space."

"You call this safe? We're in the realm of the dead, Dominic. Neither of us belongs here," I sputter, panic bleeding into the very fabric of who I am. "If we don't get back—"

The garage space around me flickers briefly, like someone trying to adjust the antenna to get a clearer picture.

His lips press into a thin line for a moment. "I know that, I do. Hell, I honestly had no idea if this was going to work for sure. I just knew it had to be done."

"So, the whole idea of leveling up was a lie?" I sputter.

Dominic chuckles, shaking his head. "No, not at all. It wasn't until I was here, until my abilities tapped into the universal energy, that I realized what needed to be done. You wanted me to help you, so that's what I'm doing."

"How in any way, shape, or form is this helping me? We could get stuck here, Dominic," I say, shoving him in the shoulder. He just chuckles at me as if it's the actions of a child. "Stop laughing. This is serious."

He shakes his head, but the movement transforms into a nod. "Yes, I know. But this was the only way to pull you outside of the earshot, so to speak, of the Moirai. They're powerful as fuck, and grounded in the land of the living. But once their job is done—meaning, once a soul has moved on—they no longer have access to it. Do you see what I'm getting at?"

"We haven't moved on," I say, alarmed at his flippant attitude.

He shakes his hands in front of him. "No, I know that. But for now, we're still outside their realm. We can talk freely here."

I narrow my gaze. "All right. So, talk already."

"Don't give me that look. Trust me, this was the only way."

I can't help but maintain my skeptical stance as I arch an eyebrow.

"Look, turns out I'm not the only one here who needed to level up. You do, too," he says. "Only you've already done it—you just don't realize it."

"What are you talking about, Dominic? We need to go." I twist around, suggesting we go...somewhere else. Only, there's no clear exit. It's all just a never-ending garage.

"Dammit, Autumn, listen to me. This is prophetic. *Divine* intervention, even." His face is deadly serious, but now it's my turn to laugh.

"You've got to be kidding me," I snicker.

"Not even a little bit," he says, taking a deep breath and stepping forward. He rests his hands along the sides of my arms and I look down, suddenly acutely aware that everything we see here isn't even real. Our actual bodies are somewhere else—and they're fading. Dominic clears his throat and continues, "You have powers no necromancer has ever had because you've been to the other side and *returned*."

"And you had to bring me here to tell me that?" I say, incredulous. "I learned that a year and a half ago. This is ridiculous."

"No, it's not," he says, dead serious. "You're not just a necromancer, Autumn. You've evolved, and you have to figure out how to embrace it so you can break your family's curse. That's what this place is telling me. It's what everything has been pointing toward—I just couldn't make sense of it."

"Evolved?" I mutter, clenching my jaw. "Into what, Dominic?"

He inhales, pinching the bridge of his nose. When he looks up, his eyes plead with me as he says, "A *sin-eater*."

I can't help it, I actually snort at him. "A *what*?"

"I didn't make up the name, for crying out loud," he says, defensively. "Look, I don't know what being a sin-eater entails, I just know you are one. And it's how you're going to break the curse. That *is* what you still want, right?"

"Of course it is," I snap.

"Then you need to learn to harness it. Whatever you did to evolve, it happened when you were a kid. Maybe that's the problem. You won't listen to me...but maybe you'll take her more seriously," Dominic says, tipping his chin upward.

I look over my shoulder, confused. Behind me, a little

girl with red hair and hazel eyes stares expectantly back at me. The girl is me—or at least, *seven year old me*.

I turn back to Dominic with wide eyes and a creepy sense of déjà vu taking over me.

"When I first saw you back at Windhaven Academy, I couldn't get the words *veritas vos liberabit* out of my head. You know this," Dominic says, raising a hand to the ceiling. "But here's the thing... I didn't know *why*. I just knew that you needed the message. Of course, I knew instantly who you were. I knew there were things you didn't know and needed to uncover. But that wasn't what it was all about. Not really."

"What do you mean?"

"Now I understand why. It's a helluva lot deeper than your family history. It was about you specifically. About who you really are—*what* you really are and what you're capable of doing," he says quietly.

"And this revelation only came to you because you 'leveled up?'" I say, shooting a sideways glance toward the little girl behind me. She's still there, waiting patiently.

"Yes," he says, point-blank. "Now, go. Get some answers. I'll be ready to go back when you are."

"But what about—?" I begin.

Dominic shrugs. "Them's the rules. You gotta get your answers before we can go back."

I groan, unable to make sense of anything he's saying. However, there's a fierce sense of curiosity and truth vibrating in the energy of the space.

"Fine," I say. Gritting my teeth, I turn back to the little girl—the younger me.

Wordlessly, she raises her right arm, extending her

hand to me. With a final glance at Dominic, I take her hand.

Instantly, the world around me shifts, falling away like a virtual reality that's been completely altered. At first, I can't see anything. It's like the entire space has been erased and I'm surrounded by nothing but a beautiful, white light that emanates a sense of peace beyond anything I can comprehend. Yet, I'm not alone. I can still feel the warmth of a small hand in mine.

As the white light pulls back, I'm suddenly in a small, dank cavern. Water fills much of the space and it drips from the ceiling, walls, and pools across the bottom of the enclosure. I don't know how I can see, since there's no light source anywhere. Yet somehow I can, but I wish I couldn't. Along the far side of the space is a stack of bodies—all children. All are in various states of decomposition. My body included.

Memories flood back to me and I'm acutely aware of the fact that this is the place where *I died*.

I remember the Vodník—the way his demeanor had changed after he got me away from the manor and the safety of my parents. He'd been so nice, telling me he'd show me a place where the mermaids lived. I'd believed him because I was trusting—too trusting.

The feeling of my soul when he had ripped it from my body, burns through my insides. He had wanted to collect it, stealing it away in his jar as a prize, just as he'd done to countless others.

I hadn't let that happen, though. Something inside me had shifted and grown more powerful by not being bound to my body. It wasn't my time yet and somehow, I knew that. I had tapped into something primal and expanded—

breaking the rules. I refused to go into his container to be a part of his collection.

In that moment of clarity, a man was at my side, entering the cavern by way of his dark, smokey portal. His silver eyes held me like a warm embrace as he took my hand, guiding my soul away from the catastrophe the Vodník had created.

Wade's father had been there—he'd been with me the day I died. He'd guided me to the other side, just as he was meant to. Only, when I got there, I couldn't let go of the intense feeling I couldn't stay. I had to return because I still had work to do.

It wasn't meant to be this way...

We had sat on the edge of the pond, dangling our feet over the edge of the dock. For some reason, he had stayed with me. I remember talking with him as if he was an old friend I hadn't seen for a long, long time.

When I told him I couldn't stay, he wasn't surprised. In fact, he seemed relieved. His expression softened as he extended his hand out between us.

In the small movement, the remaining forgotten moments blocked out in Death's presence come rushing back. My confusion, my wiped memory—all of the forgotten time had nothing to do with my parents.

It was all Death's fault.

Leaning over, the Angel of Death whispered to me, "When the time comes, this will be your most powerful weapon."

In his outstretched hand, an intricately carved wooden box materialized. The *same* wooden box gifted to me in my dad's will.

Before I have time to sit with the revelation, things

shift again. This time, I'm standing beside my father in the middle of my bedroom. He sits on my bed, staring at a picture of me. His fingertips trace my face as tears drop onto the glass's surface. My heart bursts open, and I reach for him, only to have my fingertips grasp at thin air.

Suddenly, the small resurrection room door bursts open, practically swinging off its hinges.

Dad's head jerks up. He stares at the door with wild eyes, his body trembling and his mouth agape. I turn to look at the younger version of me and she smiles, vanishing before my eyes.

As I turn back to my dad, he's on his feet, making his way to the small doorway. Fear and apprehension are splattered across his features, but he pushes through all of it, walking down the ancient wooden steps. I follow him, just as curious as he is because I have no idea what he'll find, though I should have guessed.

At the bottom of the steps, he turns the corner slowly. His eyes float to the small altar table in the center of the space. Two large pillar candles are lit, glowing brightly. Confusion flashes across his face as he walks up to it, setting down the photo frame in between them. However, just beyond, stands the young version of me. Dripping wet and shivering, she looks up at my dad with his confusion mirrored in her eyes. In her hands is the wooden box.

Without hesitation, my father races forward, practically tripping over himself to get to me. He drops to his knees at my feet, wrapping his arms around my body. As I watch, the memory of his warm arms encompassing my cold, wet body had been the most beautiful feeling in the whole world. If love had a sensation, that was it.

However, the moment wasn't meant to linger. At least, not for me.

Though my dad couldn't see him, the Angel of Death placed his hand on the back of my head—wiping my memory. He left me behind with nothing but a wooden box and a bunch of questions that would haunt me for years.

Dominic was right...I had leveled up the last time I was here. But it didn't happen alone.

It came in the form of a gift from Death himself.

CHAPTER 17
CLEAR THE SINS AWAY

As soon as the revelation of the box comes to me, a force stronger than a hurricane whisks through the memory. It wipes it away like someone clearing a drawing board and it carries me right along with it.

I try to grasp on to something, anything, to keep my bearings, but it's no use. The force sucks me into the vortex and I'm lost within in it. At first, I'm terrified, but a voice breaks the chaos telling me to *let go…*

I don't know why I should trust it, but I do. The worry and terror fade into the background and I release. I release all that I am to surrender to what is.

Whatever it is I'm *meant* to be.

For a few blissful moments, there's nothing but peace.

With a jerk, I bolt upright in the middle of the resurrection chamber, clutching at the dirt and coughing up the metallic taste of blood. Everything about the box and the Angel of Death lingers with me, holding me like a vise. I need to talk to him—demand some answers.

Beside me, Dominic rolls over, gasping for his own breath.

"It is about time," Abigail hisses, clutching at her chest as if her heart could actually beat. "I was certain I would be mourning your loss—and believe me, the irony was not lost on me."

Though her words are an admonishment, relief is clear across her face.

My mouth is dry, sucked of all moisture as I try to speak. The only word I seem able to croak out is, "Sorry."

Looking to my left, Dominic rights himself and shoots me an apologetic shrug. "So, that happened."

I narrow my gaze and ball my fist. "Ugh—" I groan, pushing him in the shoulder so he tips back over.

He clears his throat. "But it worked. Right?" His voice is just as hoarse as mine.

"Not the point," I say, scrambling to get to my feet. My body feels like lead as I struggle to stand. Everything in the realm of the dead came easier. Moving, changing space and time—it was all so much lighter. But like a dream, the memory of it fades quickly, becoming nothing more than a distant memory.

"What took you?" Abigail asks, eyeing Dominic with disdain and suspicion.

He raises his hands in the air, but stays on his ass. "Hey, I was just doing what had to be done," he protests.

Abigail's forehead creases and she turns her hard stare to me.

"As much as I hate to admit it, I think Dominic's right," I say, inhaling deeply.

Dominic's eyebrows shoot up and he points to me. "See?"

Abigail doesn't look overly amused as she presses her lips tight. However, I'm acutely aware that something has shifted. I'm even surprised she hasn't.

"Wait a minute. You can see her?" I say, turning my astonished stare on him.

He glances between me and Abigail, then nods. "Yeah, I guess I can. Before, my strongest ability was clairaudience. Looks like I have a few new tricks up my sleeve."

"Then it looks like you got what you were looking for," I say.

"Let's hope." He nods.

Abigail scrunches her face as if the idea is distasteful. "What kept you?" she repeats.

I take another deep breath, letting the memories settle. "Dominic felt I needed to join him. That there were things I needed to deal with... Abigail, what do you know about sin-eaters?" I ask, shooting a sideways glance at Dominic.

Her expression is full of confusion as she considers my words. Clasping her hands in front of her body, she paces for a few seconds before she finally says, "Rumors only. I am not even certain they exist."

"Oh, they do. And you're looking at one," Dominic says, then pointing my direction.

"Is this true?" Abigail says in a hushed whisper.

I shrug. "I don't know. That's what Dominic thinks."

"But you are not so certain?" she says, stopping her back-and-forth motion.

"I don't know anything right now. I have some questions of my own. Things are far less clear than they should be," I say, glancing quickly at Dom.

"Didn't she show you what you needed to know about it?" Dominic asks, clearly concerned.

As much as I trust both Dominic and Abigail, it doesn't feel right to talk about my time with the Angel of Death just yet. And truthfully, there was nothing about the whole sin-eating thing said at all.

Dominic must sense my apprehension, because he narrows his gaze.

"No, she didn't," I say. It's not a lie, but it's certainly not the whole truth, either. Turning back to Abigail, I say, "What can you tell me about sin-eaters?"

Abigail's eyes go distant for a few seconds, but something in her demeanor changes. It's almost hopeful. "Sin-eaters are said to do just that, consume the sins of another."

I never was one for religious context, and I feel myself already recoiling from the idea of what the subtext suggests. "What does that mean?"

Abigail shakes her head solemnly.

"*What?*" I say, spitting out the word more forcefully than I intended.

She looks to Dominic, as if somehow he might be able to help her put into words whatever a sin-eater actually is. Despite his normal bravado, he remains relatively stoic as his gaze drops casually to the sandy floor. Rather than participate in what is evidently a family discussion, he backs up slowly, resting his shoulders along the stone wall.

I roll my eyes at his helpfulness.

"I don't know the exact methodology," Abigail says, her voice grave. "But from what I have gathered, it would mean you take on the sins of another. They become your own."

"Well, so what? That doesn't sound so bad," I say.

Abigail's eyebrows tug in and she nods. "Perhaps."

"There's a downside. That's what Abigail's trying to say," Dominic offers.

"Of course there is," I say, exhaling loudly.

"Everything is about balance. Good and evil. Light and dark. Should you take on the sins of another, it would be a mark against your soul. It becomes a part of you as if you did the sinning yourself," Abigail begins. "And as you can see, some sins have consequences. Painful, long-lasting consequences, even."

"Hmmm," I mutter.

"This is not the sort of gift you would wish to take lightly," Abigail says. "Should this be true, I implore you to deliberate long and hard on how to best perform these duties."

I step away from her, trying to sort out the information I've been given.

If I were to embrace this idea—being a sin-eater—does this mean I can clear away the past transgressions of the family? Is this the curse-breaker we've been searching for? Could I clear away the sins of Abigail and Warren? And if so, does that mean she would finally be free to cross over?

But more than that, would it free the rest of us? What about Wade? Myself... *The baby?*

And if the answer is yes, then where do I sign up?

"Did you know about this?" I ask, turning to face Abigail again. "That I could become a sin-eater?"

Surprise flits through her face and she takes a step back. "I held some suspicions, but I could not be certain."

"Why?" I say, holding my breath as I wait for her answer.

"Autumn, you have always been powerful. Very, very powerful. As a child, you were but one with forces our family has never been able to command before. You could see and speak to me. Something not many can do." She raises an eyebrow at Dominic, who grins in return and crosses his arms over his chest. "It wasn't until I realized your mother was hiding aspects of who she was..." her voice peters out and she looks at me from under her eyebrows.

"You mean the fact that she has powers, too?" I say.

For once, it's nice to know something when others are tiptoeing around it.

Her face brightens. "Yes. Precisely."

"Wait. Your mom has powers?" Dominic says, surprise etched into the lines of his face as he drops his arms and stands up straight.

I nod.

"Huh, that explains a lot," he mutters under his breath.

"At first I believed your mother to be of ordinary nature. Yet, there were times when I could swear she sensed me. It was, of course, after the accident that I learned of her origin," Abigail whispers, dropping her chin to her chest. She eyes her fingertips for a moment as if they're far more interesting than anything she's saying.

"When I first moved back, do you remember the first thing you told me?" I ask her.

The place between her eyebrows creases as she thinks.

Rather than wait for her answer, I continue, "You told me I had to break the curse. That I'm the only one who can release you from this binding." I pause, watching her reaction.

Her lips press tightly, but she nods.

"At the time, I didn't want to hear any of it. It was all still so new. You know?" I say, remembering back to that day. "It was a lot to take in."

"I can imagine," she says.

"Did you mean it? That you thought I could break the curse?"

She clasps her hands behind her back and straightens her shoulders. "I have grown very fond of you, child."

"Is that a yes or a no?" I spit, suddenly frustrated by her cryptic manner.

A surprisingly pained expression takes over her features and she sighs. "I had *hoped*...I knew you were different and you are the remaining Blackwood. So, if anyone was to break the curse, it would be you. Otherwise, the Moirai win. Our family dies out with you and I'm trapped in this limbo forever."

"Not exactly," I say, swallowing hard.

Abigail's expression changes to confusion, and I smile softly. It really is nice to be the one in the know. "I'm pregnant, Abigail."

"No—" she breathes, anguish clear in her eyes.

"Yes," I say, suddenly alarmed by her fervor.

Dominic nods. "It's true. I've sensed it myself."

"Should the Moirai learn of this, they will want to act quickly," she says, suddenly standing directly in front of me. "This is far more dangerous than I feared."

"What are you talking about?"

"Think about it, child. If you are to stop the curse, you must do so before the Moirai catch on to this turn of events. They will be called in soon to set the course for this child. His or her string will be woven and..." Her voice trails off as she walks away from me. "You must put an end to this curse as quickly as possible. Through which means, I am not certain. But should you decide to ascend to a sin-eater, you cannot perform these rites when there is a child growing inside of you."

I shake my head, not following her logic. "Why not?"

"You could inadvertently beset *the child* with the burden of those sins. No innocent life should ever come into this world afflicted with such torment," she says, reaching out to me. Her arms hover beside mine, clearly wanting to touch me but knowing she's unable. "I will not allow it. There has to be another way."

I stumble backward, shaking my head. "That can't be right."

If Dom is right, and this is what I'm meant to become, why would I only learn about it when I can't do anything about it?

My phone springs to life, shocking adrenaline through my system and pulling me from the horrible revelation Abigail just shared. When I realize it's my mom, my heart jumps into my throat as I fumble to answer.

"Hello?" I sputter, trying to stay calm.

"Sweetie, I think you better get back here," she says.

"What's happened? What's wrong?" I ask, my words tumbling out in a cluster.

"Things have gotten worse." She pauses for a moment "The doctors are concerned Wade may not make it through the night," she says, her voice as gentle as silk as she tries to soften the blow. "I'm so sorry, Autumn. I wish there was something I could do."

I pull the phone back, staring at it, unable to process fully what she just said. Without thinking, I hang up the phone, and the entire world feels like it falls away. It doesn't matter who else needs me or what needs to be done.

Forget curses. Sin-eaters. The Moirai. Forget all of it.

"We'll have to deal with this later," I say, shooting Abigail and Dominic a significant look. Neither one of them raise an objection. "You're gonna need to find your way home, Dominic. I gotta...*go*."

With that, I race up the stairs, leaving the resurrection room behind. I don't stop when I reach my bedroom, either. I keep running, grabbing my keys and heading straight out the door of the manor.

If I was speeding before, it'll be nothing like this time.

Hang on, Wade. I'm coming. Please, please hang on.

CHAPTER 18
RIPPLES

My mind circles all of the recent events—Wade, the mark, the pregnancy, Dominic, the realm of the dead, and the strange box given to me by the Angel of Death.

Intense anger rolls through me and I slam the palm of my hand against the steering wheel.

The Angel of Death...

How could he do this to Wade? Why would he allow this to happen to him? And why would he keep so much from me? We've met before? He gave me the mysterious box? Hell, he must have known things were going to go sideways at some point... What else does he know?

My lips press tight, but I can't hold back the rage.

"Where are you, you bastard?" I call out. My ears ring as the words echo around the small cab space of the Ford Escape. "Wade is sick because of you. He could be *dying*. Why aren't you doing anything to stop it?" I hold my breath, half-expecting him to materialize on the seat beside me. When he doesn't, I continue. "This is absolute bullshit, you know. Wade doesn't deserve this."

Despite my anger, he doesn't answer my admonishment. Instead, I'm left to stew in my anger, worry, and sorrow. But he's not going to get away from this that easy. Oh hell no, we're going to mix words.

How I manage to arrive at the hospital without getting pulled over is a complete mystery to me. The entire drive from Windhaven to Mistwood is a total blur as I skid into the hospital parking lot.

The beating in my chest has reached a fever pitch and I hope like hell that Wade's hung on for me.

Slamming Blue into park, I rush from the vehicle and into the hospital. Mom is right where I left her in the waiting area, and as soon as she sees me, she stands up and rushes over.

"Oh, sweetie. I'm so sorry," she says, wrapping her arms around me.

"How is he?" I ask, scared to death to hear her answer.

She pulls back, tugging me into a chair beside her, as she takes a seat. "He's stable, but not well. They can tell that whatever is happening is supernatural in nature, but they've never seen anything like it, so they're not sure how to treat it."

I raise my eyebrows. "They probably haven't seen a helluva lot of expulsion marks from the Angel of Death."

She shakes her head. "Not at all."

"Can I see him? Will they let me in there?" I ask, desperation filling my tone.

"I think so," she nods. "Let me see what I can do."

With that, she gets up, marching herself over to the receptionist. The lady who was there when I first got here is gone and in her place is a man with cropped black hair and dark skin. As Mom approaches, he grins wide at her. I watch the exchange with bated breath, hoping like hell this guy will be more helpful than the last person.

"Thanks, Gary," Mom says, her voice carrying across the space. She taps the countertop and spins around, giving me the thumbs up as she approaches.

"So, they'll let me in?" I say, shooting to my feet.

"Give them a second. Gary has to go find the doctor on call," she says. "But he seemed to think they can get you in there."

I exhale in relief, but I'm too nervous to sit back down. Instead, I pace back and forth, waiting for someone to come out and talk to me.

Finally, a woman in a bright-white smock comes out of the locked doors beyond, clipboard in hand. Her black hair is piled in a messy bun on the top of her head, giving the impression she's much taller than she actually is.

"Ms. Blackwood?" she asks, eyeing me for confirmation.

I extend my hand and nod. "Yes."

She shakes my hand and nods to herself. "It's nice to meet you. I'm Dr. Lockstad, the attending physician. I understand you are Mr. Hoffman's girlfriend?" she says, flipping through the paperwork on her clipboard.

"I am," I say, trying not to sound too abrupt. "But I'm the closest thing he has to family."

"I see," she says, clearly stalling as she reads more of his paperwork.

Surely it has to say his family is gone.

My mom stands up, placing her hand along my back in support.

"Well, our hospital policy is that only next of kin—"

"With all due respect, I don't give a damn about the hospital policy, Dr. Lockstad. I'm not letting the father of my child go through this alone," I say. "I need to be with him."

Her dark-brown eyes widen, and she lowers her voice. "The two of you share a child?"

"Not yet, but we will," I say, my hands falling to my stomach. "I'm pregnant."

She inhales slowly. Though her eyes hold a hint of suspicion, she nods. "All right. Come with me to his room. We can go over some of the details. Of course, some things will have to be confidential unless he wakes up and authorizes more."

"Understood. As long as I can be near him, that's what matters."

"I'll give you two some space," Mom says, leaning in and kissing the side of my cheek. "I'll run home and grab a few things for you. Is there anything specific you want?"

I shake my head, unable to think about anything I need more than Wade right now.

"Okay, well, call me if you do. I won't be gone long," she says.

I nod, reaching for my keys and handing them over to her. "I will."

With that, Mom heads out the door and the doctor tilts her head toward the intensive care ward. "So, Wade is doing better, but we aren't certain how to treat him. The infection is spreading and his body is working overtime to try to fight it off," Dr. Lockstad says, leading the way beyond the double doors.

"My mom made it sound like he had gotten worse. Is that not the case?" I say, watching her closely.

Her forehead creases and she winces slightly. "He goes through unusual episodes. One moment, he's stable and comfortable. Then, the next his heart rate and temp spike. He almost seizes. It's had the nurses in a panic more than once."

My eyes widen and all I can think to say is, "Oh."

"What do you know about the mark on his chest?" she asks.

"Honestly, not much. His father gave it to him a couple of months ago."

Concern flits through her features and she makes a face. "I thought you said his family was gone?"

"I—they are. Wade's an unusual supernatural," I say, running my fingertips along my forehead. "His father is the Angel of Death."

Her dark eyes widen and her lips transform into the shape of an O. "Well, that explains a few things."

"It does?" I ask.

Dr. Lockstad stops and faces me. "The mark has an ouroboros, and we were trying to understand its significance."

"A what?" I say, tugging my eyebrows in.

"An ouroboros. A snake eating its tail. In some mythologies it symbolizes the cycle of birth and death. But the circle can also mean protection, too. So, the fact that it was snakelike had us a bit confounded," she says. "I'll make sure to pass this information along to our supernatural team right away."

"Good," I say, hoping like hell this new information is beneficial to them.

"Well, this is his room. He seems pretty comfortable again, but don't be surprised if he goes into another one of his episodes. It seems to happen more and more frequently," she says, patting my shoulder and walking away.

I turn to face the small window on his door. For some reason, I'm suddenly scared to open the door. I want to see him back to normal—back to the way he should be.

All of this is my fault. Had I kept my distance, none of this would have happened. The Moirai wouldn't be after him. His father wouldn't have expelled him.

He wouldn't be fighting for his life.

I swallow hard and push open the door. My heart thuds awkwardly as I move closer, practically tiptoeing to Wade's bed. He doesn't look well. Instead of the usual soft wave in his dark hair that brushes over his left eye, his hair is matted against his forehead. The rosy color of his cheeks is practically gone, replaced by an eerie pale white, like all of his blood has somehow hidden itself deep under the surface.

An IV is hooked up to his wrist and a small tube vanishes into one of his nostrils.

When I reach him, tears cloud my vision, and I can't stop my chin from trembling. For the longest time, I stand there, watching him through the tears and listening to the metronome of his heart monitor as I try to regain some composure.

A small v forms between his eyebrows and I wish like hell I could take the pain away for him.

"Wade, I'm so sorry. I wish there was something—" My words get stuck in my throat and I clamp my mouth shut. Instead, I reach out, taking his hand in mine. His skin is cold and clammy, but there's no way I'd ever want to let it go.

With my foot, I tug the small hospital chair closer, and I take a seat at his bedside.

It's almost as if hospitals are portals to a realm where all time slows down. For what seems like days, I sit there, vaguely aware of the ticking of the clock and the beeping of the machines monitoring Wade's condition.

Every once in a while, someone wanders in, checking on Wade's vitals. They smile apologetically at me and leave as quickly as they come.

The only saving grace is the fact that Wade seems more relaxed than before. The crease in his forehead has diminished a bit and luckily, he hasn't had any of his episodes.

I lean forward, resting my head on the edge of the bed. But I no sooner set my forehead against the blanket than I hear the door to the room open.

I glance up and find Mom walking into the room.

"Here's your backpack, sweetie. It has some essentials in it. Clothes, toothbrush, that sort of thing. I even dropped a few snacks in there in case you get hungry," she says, shooting me her worried-mom face. She passes the backpack to me and I set it on the floor by my feet.

"Thanks, Mom. I appreciate it," I say, trying to smile.

Her lips curve upward slightly, and she walks to the other side of Wade's bed. Placing a hand over his, she looks up at me. "How is he doing?"

I shake my head. "I don't know. It's been relatively quiet since I got in here. They keep checking his vitals, but he hasn't really moved or anything."

"That's the hardest part, for sure. The waiting," Mom

says.

I nod.

"Are you hungry? Do you want to get a bite to eat in the cafeteria before they close up for the night?" she asks, eyeing me. "We never got to eat our turkey, and I'd be surprised if you ate anything after you left."

I shake my head. "I'm not hungry."

"Autumn, you need to keep up your strength. Besides, you're not just eating for you." She tips her chin toward me and raises her eyebrows.

She's right, I know she is. But I don't want to leave his side.

As if sensing my apprehension, Mom says, "How about this... I'll run down and get us something to eat. You stay here and keep an eye on things. Deal?"

Relief spreads through me and I nod. "Yeah, that would be better."

She winks at me and without another word, she walks out. Time spreads out again while she's gone, and I find myself unable to keep my eyes open while I wait.

I drop my head again to the side of the bed, resting my forehead beside our hands.

Focusing on the hospital noises, my body is suddenly drifting...

Once again, I'm sitting on the edge of the dock.

My bare feet splash in the cool water, and I can't help but feel somewhat happy in the way the water droplets cascade across the surface. They ripple outward, interacting with each other the way we ripple across the lives of those we meet.

Suddenly, the Angel of Death is by my side and I'm once again seven years old.

"Big things are coming your way. You know that, right?" he says to me. His words are soft, spoken the way a kindergarten teacher speaks to her students.

"I suppose," I say, unsure what response he's looking for. In my hands is the wooden box he'd given me. For some reason, I can't stop staring at its unique carvings. "What does this do?"

"There is plenty of time to puzzle on that," he says, smiling softly.

"That doesn't help, you know," I say, frowning.

He chuckles. "Understanding its purpose isn't all that hard, Autumn," he says, his voice still soft and deliberate. "You just need to read its inscription and it will tell you everything you need to know."

I wake up with a jolt.

Beside me, Wade's forehead is beaded with sweat and his lips have taken on a bluish tinge. I feel absolutely useless. There's nothing I can do to help him—but I can't just sit here and wait, either.

Inhaling sharply, I glance down at my open backpack. The box is tilted on its side, half-buried by my sweatshirt. Reaching it, I pull it out, turning it over in my hand.

Maybe Mom was right about the sigils. I wish I'd had more time to look into it. Along the edges, there are markings that look like words from some sort of long-lost language. I continue to turn it over, eyeing it from every angle.

If the inscription is the key...

How in the hell do I figure out how to read the damn thing?

CHAPTER 19
MERRY CHRISTMAS

The etchings on the outside of the box make absolutely no sense in my brain. But in a strange way, the longer I stare at them, the more they remind me of a combination of hieroglyphics and modern-day Chinese. Beyond that, it's like no kind of writing I've ever seen. Yet, my mom seems to think that's what it is. Assuming she's right, and assuming the dream was real, I need to learn what this means. *Fast*.

If I could just understand why the Angel of Death gave me the box, or hell, *wiped my memory*, maybe things would start to make sense. I wish Wade was better so he could make his dad come to us, since the Angel of Death clearly doesn't answer to me at all. Of course, that's only one of the many reasons I wish Wade was better.

Setting the box aside, I lean forward and pick up Wade's hand. His palm is cool and almost clammy, but as soon as our skin touches, he sighs. It's as if he's somehow aware of my touch and it comforts him. At the very least, it lightens my heart to know that even in this state, even in whatever pain he must be in, I bring him a little bit of peace. I only wish this wasn't all my fault.

"You should have stayed away from me," I whisper, stroking the edge of his thumb with my pointer finger. As much as I knew it—as much as he knew it—we just couldn't seem to do the safe thing.

Wade groans, arching his back slightly.

I run my hand across his forearm, but his face crumples and his head tips backward. He practically buries the top of his head in the pillow as his torso lifts off the bed. Suddenly, the monitor with his heart rate shows a sharp spike and the rest of the machines all around us spring to life.

Still holding his hand, I kick my chair back, letting it skid across the tile floor. Before I can make any other moves, two nurses rush in from the hallway.

"Take a step back, please," one of them says, sliding between me and the bed. Her arm is forceful as she practically knocks me back.

I clutch at the edge of the deep window well, staring in horror as the two of them hover over Wade. The second nurse rotates away from him, turning to the readouts from the heart machine and checking them over.

The next thing I know, Doctor Lockstad hurries in. She marches straight to Wade, but there's no hint of panic in her face at all. It's as if, at this point, she's used to whatever this is. In some small way, it takes a bit of the edge off my own panic. Her eyes narrow as she pulls out a small pen light and lifts his eyelids, shining the light in his eyes with a quick flick of her wrist.

"He needs his next round of steroids and some sedation. Make sure his fluid intake is increased as well," she says to the nurse who took my place at the bedside.

"On it," she says, nodding to the doctor and pivoting to one of the plastic bin units beside the bed. She pulls out a number of medical supplies, then exits the room quickly. When she comes back, she has a couple of small vials in her hand.

Dr. Lockstad slowly checks over Wade's vitals as he flails hard against her. "Hang tight here, Wade. It'll be all over soon," she says, her voice calm and steady.

It doesn't seem like he hears her at all. He continues to arch his back, rocking from side to side as if fighting an imaginary beast. Then, one of his arms flies up to the mark on his chest. He claws at his hospital gown, tugging at it until the gown releases slightly, revealing angry red lines surrounding the mark. The black webbing is etched deeper into his skin, like a poison trying to infect the rest of his body.

The nurse who had been checking the machine readouts grabs his arms, trying to keep them down.

"Where are we at with the restraints?" Dr. Lockstad asks, her forehead now a cluster of concern.

"I'm sorry. The ward has been so crazy today. You know how it is on Christmas. I'll go get them now," the nurse responds.

As she disappears down the hall, I step up, grabbing onto Wade's wrists and holding them so he can't hurt himself. My thoughts are a tangled mess, but I can't help but be surprised by the single word. "Restraints? Are you sure that's necessary? He's been so quiet up until now," I say, struggling to keep his arms down.

The nurse hands the doctor a needle.

"Just until we can get these episodes under control," Dr. Lockstad says, injecting the medication into Wade's IV. The nurse hands her a second injection and she goes through the motion all over again.

It takes a few minutes for whatever they gave him to work, but I can tell the instant it does. The rigidity of his muscles relaxes and the fight left in his arms dwindles.

"It's okay, Wade. We're here," I whisper, removing my right hand to run it across his cheek. "I'm here."

He sighs, his forehead relaxing slightly.

"He knows you're here," Dr. Lockstad says, her lips turning up slightly.

"I wish I could do more," I say, refusing to divert my gaze from his face.

How could we have come this far? This morning he was fine. More than fine, he was *perfect*. And I was just about to tell him about the pregnancy...

I'd give anything to be back at that point. I wish I had told him.

The nurse who left to find restraints returns, holding them up for all to see. "Found some down on the third floor."

"See, he's calmed down now. Does he really need those?" I ask, wishing I could throw them in the trash.

"It's for his own safety. If he strains himself too much or claws at his skin before we can make it in here..." Dr. Lockstad begins, her voice trailing off.

"I'm not going anywhere. If that's all it is, I'll be here to keep him from harming himself," I say, pleading with her with my eyes. "It's the least I can do."

Dr. Lockstad shifts her gaze from me, to Wade, then

back again. She sighs. "All right. If you think you can handle this task, we'll give it a try."

I tip my head and exhale in relief. "Thank you."

"But if it gets to be too much..." Dr. Lockstad warns.

I nod. "Then I know what comes next."

She smiles warily at me but dips her chin.

The nurse's arms drop to her side, and she walks over to one of the cupboards on her right. "I'll place them in here, just in case."

The doctor nods at her but turns back to Wade. She checks him over once more, running through what looks like a well-worn sequence of checkpoints. As he relaxes back into a quiet state, I pull my hands from his arms and stand up straighter. My fingertips trace his arm, floating back to his hand.

"You will not believe how long the lines were down there. I had to fight off an old lady for the last bit of turkey...." Mom says, entering the room with a tray stacked high with an assortment of food and drinks. As soon as she takes in the scene, her eyes widen and she says, "What's happened?"

I shake my head, holding back tears. Now that the danger has passed, the emotions swelling from the day's events are ready to sweep me away. I don't know how much more I can take.

"Just a little episode. We should be good for a while now," Dr. Lockstad says, catching the eye of the nurses. With a quick head tilt toward the door, they excuse themselves and walk out. "Looks like you have some dinner plans. I'll let the two of you relax a bit." She pats my mom on the shoulder as she walks by.

"Thank you, Dr. Lockstad," Mom says, but her eyes

never leave me. When the door closes behind them, Mom asks, "Are you okay?"

I exhale a jagged breath, my eyes straying over to Wade. "Yeah, it was just...intense. He's really fighting against whatever this is. I don't know what to do. Or how to help him."

"Was the situation with Dominic a bust?" Mom says, making her way to me.

"I don't know, to be honest," I say, shaking my head. I don't know how much to tell her without freaking her out. "It was weird."

Mom pulls a small fold-out table from a cubby in the wall and tips her chin. "Wanna help with this? Then tell me all about it."

Doing as she asks, I walk over to the small table, lifting the tabletop up and snapping it into place. She sets the tray down and starts divvying up the items. "Well, it's not quite the Christmas Eve dinner I had in mind, that's for sure," she says, placing the tray on the floor.

"That makes two of us." I smile absently, shooting another glance at Wade.

Whatever fight was left in him has gone and he's sunk back into the bed. I walk up to him, running the back of my hand across his jawline. I pull up the fabric from his hospital gown, then walk to my chair and tug it closer to the table. Mom grabs a second chair from across the room and does the same.

"Try the turkey. Hopefully it was worth the effort," Mom says, clearly trying to keep things light.

Despite her best efforts, I just can't seem to muster much enthusiasm for food. I push my plastic fork around the plate as I stare at the gelatinous potatoes and gravy.

"So, tell me, what happened with Dominic?" Mom asks, taking a bite of her turkey and making a face. She sets her fork down and opens a small plastic bag with cornbread inside.

I lean back in my chair, still a little apprehensive to be talking openly about any of this. After all these years, it's hard to get past her previous aversion to anything in this supernatural world.

As if sensing my trepidation, she says, "I won't bite. I promise." She makes an x across her heart with her index finger.

I smile feebly, but after a brief pause, I say, "Dominic believes I'm a sin-eater."

Her eyes widen and it's clear instantly—the word means something to her.

Rather than having her interject just yet, I continue, "The only problem is, if I act on this idea, Abigail thinks I would be putting the baby in danger." I poke at the green beans on the divided plate.

Mom's eyebrows pucker in the middle and she leans forward. "And this is meant to help Wade somehow?"

I shake my head and shrug. "Honestly, I don't know. It was all mixed up in messages about the Moirai's curse. He seemed to think it was the key to ending it all. But the curse isn't even what I'm worried most about right now. *Obviously.*"

"Hmmm," she says, tapping at the table with her fingertips.

"What is it?" I ask, narrowing my gaze.

Her hazel eyes flash with intensity. "Maybe nothing."

"No, you can't do that. Spill it," I say, lowering my eyebrows.

She stands up, walking over to Wade's bedside. With her right hand, she pulls back the fabric of his hospital gown. "I've been thinking a lot about this. You said it was a mark of expulsion, right?"

I nod. "That's what the Angel of Death said."

Her lips press into a thin line and she shakes her head. "It's just not sitting right with me."

"Why?" I ask, setting my fork down.

She inhales slowly. "I don't know of any parent who would *actively* put their child in harm's way. Not any decent one, anyhow."

"I don't think he had a choice," I mutter. "He was pretty clear that necromancers and Angels of Death were unmixy things."

"Hmmm," she repeats, her eyes distant.

Her questions and thought process spark a new hope inside of me. What if the Angel of Death saw this coming? Whatever *this* is. And if she's right...maybe that means his father put in a safeguard. Something that might help me save Wade after all.

"So, what are you thinking then?" I ask.

She walks back to me, sitting down in her chair. "I'm not sure yet. But I'll do some digging."

Exhaling slowly, I nod. As much as I hope his father wouldn't do this to hurt Wade, I also know what it looks like. If appearances tell the whole story, it would look like his father's mark is the cause of all of this. But if it is, something doesn't add up... Why would he give me that box?

"Mom, before all this happened...you mentioned the box looked like it had writing on it. Do you know how I could find out what it says?" I ask.

"I know a few people who can still read the old languages. I could ask around," she says, eyeing me carefully. "Do you know where it is?"

I nod, standing up. "Yeah, it was in the backpack you brought me." I walk over to it, reaching for the box and passing it to her.

Mom takes it, turning it over slowly and examining it from a few angles. "I'd like to take a few pictures, if you don't mind. I can email them off and see what they think. We probably won't hear back until tomorrow, though," she says, scrunching her face.

"Tomorrow is good. I'm completely at a loss right now," I say, inhaling deeply. "But I think there's something important about the box. Maybe something that will help Wade."

"It's quite puzzling, isn't it?" she whispers, pulling her phone out of her pocket and holding the box up. She snaps a few pictures from all different angles. When she's satisfied, she hands the box back to me.

I clutch it to my chest, wishing I knew what the hell it was all about. What is so important that the Angel of Death wanted me to have it—but forget it existed at the same time?

Mom stifles a yawn with the back of her hand.

"Why don't you head home, Mom? It's been a long, horrible day. Get some rest," I say. "No reason we both have to be here."

She shakes her head. "No, no. I can stay here with you, Autumn. You shouldn't be alone."

"I'm not alone," I say, reaching again for Wade's hand.

"What about supper?" she asks, pointing at our uneaten meals.

"I'm not really all that hungry," I mutter, making a face.

"Figured as much. I suppose I should do something with our turkey at home. I turned it way down when I went back, but it should be done soon," she says, obviously losing the internal battle to stay here. "Is there anything you need? Anything I can do before I go?"

I shake my head. "No. Just see if you can figure out what the box says."

"Okay, sweetie. I'll bring back some real turkey tomorrow, too," she says, sticking out her tongue at the small foldout table.

"That sounds great," I say, smiling weakly. "I should be more hungry then, too."

She takes a deep breath, shoving her phone in her pocket. Rounding the end of the bed, she walks up to me and wraps her arms around my shoulders. "Please keep your strength up. Eat something—not the dinner, but a muffin or something. I'll leave it all here."

"Okay," I chuckle under my breath.

She kisses the top of my head, her hand sliding inside my own. With a quick squeeze, she turns on her heel to leave. As she reaches the door, she turns back and says, "Hang in there, Wade. See you in the morning, Autumn."

"Okay, Mom," I say, waving. "Merry Christmas."

"Merry Christmas, sweetheart," she says, trying not to frown. With a quick tug, she opens the door and walks out.

Suddenly alone, the weight of the day bears down on me. Its oppressive energy is almost more than I can handle. Tears brim at the edges of my eyes, tipping over and painting my cheeks. I drop to my knees beside Wade's bed, clutching at his hand.

I've never been the praying type, but I'd pray to every god, goddess, or celestial being if I thought just one of them might hear my plight and take notice. For the longest time, I stay there, letting my legs go numb from the cold tile floor. With every fiber of my being I wish I could do something—change it all. Take all this pain away and make everything right.

All of a sudden, the door to Wade's room opens. I tip my chin upward.

The shifts must have changed because a new nurse walks in, shooting me a reluctant smile. Her chocolate hair is pinned up in a loose bun at the back of her head, making the white of her uniform stand out in deep contrast. Even the other nurses had a little color to their garb.

"Hello," she says curtly as she closes the door quietly behind her. She walks over to the machines, looking over the readings that hold the details of Wade's current condition.

I swallow hard, wiping at my face as I try to regain some composure.

"This must be hard for you," the nurse says, not even turning to look at me.

"You could say that," I whisper.

She continues to work, flitting between machines. Then, when she looks like she's satisfied, she turns to Wade. Holding onto the rail of his bed, she tilts her head slightly to the side, watching him for the longest time.

"Such a pity," she finally says, breaking the silence.

I glance over at her, fighting back the tears still threatening to emerge. "You have no idea."

She considers my words for a moment but silently nods.

I close my eyes, hoping she leaves soon so I can be alone with Wade again.

"Sweetie, is this yours?" the nurse asks.

Opening my eyes, she extends her hand to me.

Confused, I reach out to accept whatever it is she's found. I don't remember dropping anything, but who knows in all of the commotion from earlier.

However, from her outstretched palm falls a single tattered red thread.

CHAPTER 20
LACHESIS

Panic races through me and for a moment, I'm frozen solid with my arm still extended above Wade's torso. When I look up, the nurse's golden eyes flash mischievously, and a hint of a smile paints the edges of her lips.

"Who are you?" I demand, crumpling my hand around the string.

"I think you already have a fairly decent hypothesis. So, with that in mind, I'd like to hear your theory first," she says, dropping her gaze from me to Wade. Slowly, she runs her left index finger down his exposed arm.

"Don't touch him," I spit.

She shoots me a look of admonishment. "If I was here to hurt him, do you really think there's anything *you* could do to stop me?"

My heart thumps unevenly and my torso feels like it's been hollowed out. "Then *why* are you here?"

Her gaze drops to Wade's shoulder, and she pulls his hospital gown down a couple more inches. Her forehead creases as she takes in the mark on his chest. "Not even *Death* can cheat *Fate*," she mutters. "You'd think he'd know that by now."

"Wade didn't do this—" I sputter.

"Not *him*," she says, clearly agitated as she glares back at me.

"Then who—?" The question cuts off in the back of my throat and I look back down at Wade's mark and it's suddenly clear. "His father," I whisper.

"It's no wonder we've been having problems with his thread," she whispers, tipping her chin up and inspecting the mark a little more closely. "Nice handiwork, though, I have to admit. He knew what he was doing. The ouroboros is a nice touch."

"It's a mark of expulsion. His father banished him," I say, feeling like I need to somehow defend Wade from her discerning gaze.

A soft chuckle escapes her lips and she looks over to me. "Is that what he told you?"

I narrow my eyes, unsure if she's trying to mislead me or if she's genuinely this obnoxious. "No, I made it up myself," I spit back, making a face.

"Well, you were lied to. This mark here has one purpose only," she says, her left eyebrow arching high as she presses her finger to Wade's skin. "To hide his thread from us. I'll admit, it did take a few more resources than ordinary to locate him." She suddenly snaps her thumb and index finger together. Her clothes change from a standard nurse's garb to a pristine white pantsuit.

My mouth drops open and I blink back in disbelief.

It's not a mark of expulsion?

I take a step back, reeling from the news. Clearly, my mother was right...

But why would his father lie to us?

"Which one are you?" I ask, swallowing hard.

Again, she places her golden eyes on me, letting her gaze creep over me like a spider hunting for its prey. "Lachesis," she says, lifting her chin almost defiantly.

A shiver rolls through me to hear her name out loud. Wade and I had studied the Fates last semester, but to learn you're staring into the face of Fate—or at least one of them—is a bit much.

"You're the middle sister, right?" I say, remembering my research.

She shrugs nonchalantly. "We were all created at the same time."

We stare at each other from across the bed. For a moment, we're at an impasse. I don't know what she wants, but I'm scared to death to find out. On the other hand, I'm sure one way or another, ignoring her isn't an option.

"My sisters and I have our places. It really doesn't matter which one is first, second, or third. Without all three, reality falls apart," Lachesis says, patting the edge of Wade's bed and stepping away. "Chaos ensues."

"So, if you're not here to hurt us...why are you here?" I say, clutching on to Wade's hand.

"Come on, Autumn. You're not this naive." Deep grooves appear on her forehead as she frowns at me.

I shake my head. "What are you talking about?"

"I'm not here for him, for starters. I'm here to talk to you," Lachesis says.

My heart skips a beat and I almost drop Wade's hand

to take a step back. "You're here for me?" My words are breathless as my free hand drops to my abdomen.

"Don't worry. I'm not here to claim you, either," she says. "I just want to talk."

I narrow my eyes, instantly suspicious.

"Do you honestly think most people get the hints I've been dropping?" she asks, raising a hand in the air. "Your family is special. It always has been. Truth be told, I was rooting for your dad. Too bad he picked the wrong sister." She makes a face and does a strange sort of jazz hands effect.

"What do you mean?" I ask, narrowing my eyes.

She tips her head back, staring at the false ceiling and fluorescent lighting for a few seconds. "I shouldn't even be telling you this, but I'm so damned tired of having to keep score."

"Okay..."

Lachesis walks over to the folding table and picks through the leftover food. She finds a small cookie and holds it up. "Do you mind?"

I shake my head. "Uh, no. Help yourself."

Grinning, she rips open the bag and tears a bit off. She pops it in her mouth as she walks back over to the bed. "Everyone thinks when it comes to us, the one they need to appeal to is Aisa—she's the ones with the shears, after all. *I get it.* They think that if they offer her something, beg her to reconsider, she can somehow alter the course of what has already been set into motion..."

"But...?" I ask, hanging onto every word she says despite myself.

"But," she says, tearing off another chunk of the cookie, "of the three of us, Aisa is the *only* one who's locked into her orders. Why do you think she's called the *Unforgiving One*? I mean, come on?"

"But you're different?" I ask.

"Clotho and I, well...we've both grown restless in the predictability of our roles. We have a tendency to root for the underdogs every now and again," she says, winking at me. "Once in a while, there's a particular family who captures our attention. Yours happens to be one of them."

"I'm not following..." I say, trying to read the nuances in between what she's saying, but I'm afraid if I do, I'll read her wrong and screw everything up.

"Look, I know what you're going to try to do...and I have to admit, I'm impressed," she says, walking around the end of the bed toward me.

"I don't know what you're talking about," I say, clamping my mouth shut.

Her face goes deadpan and she blinks back at me slowly. "Don't patronize me, dear. I'm the epitome of destiny. Who do you think *finds* these loopholes in the tapestry of life?"

I inhale sharply. "You're talking about me *evolving*."

A smile breaks out across her face. "Is that what we're calling it?"

I press my lips tight, waiting for her to continue.

"So, here's the thing," she says, pressing her palms together. "Clotho and I... Well, we approve."

My heart practically stops. Dropping Wade's hand, I walk around his bedside, pulling her away from where he rests. "You approve? Of me becoming a *sin-eater*?"

Saying the word out loud still feels strange.

"Yes," she says matter-of-factly.

My fingertips fly upward, and I press them hard against

my forehead. The idea of evolving into a sin-eater was meant to be a surprise to the Moirai, not the other way around.

"There's just one thing," she says, her golden gaze glued to me.

"Of course there is," I mutter, almost scared to find out.

"If you're to do this, you can't wait. The threads have been measured for each of you already and they're beginning to fray. Your friend's father knew that." She eyes me knowingly. "Once Aisa has her orders, there will be no stopping her."

"What about my child? If I do this," I sputter, remembering what Abigail had said.

"That is a dilemma, I'm not going to lie," she says. "Becoming a sin-eater means accepting the past regressions of those you take on. It affects you, body and soul, until you are brought to the gates of judgement. When your body is a shared entity..."

"I won't do that to my child," I sputter, shaking my head and backing away.

"There is a way..." Lachesis says, shooting me a sideways glance. Her eyes flicker with a glow all their own.

"What is it?" I ask breathlessly.

She leans in closer. "Sin-eaters typically deal in the land of the living. Everyone has sins they need to atone for. When sin-eaters take on the sins of others, they do it so they do not suffer into the afterlife. So their lineage does not suffer and curses aren't born." Lachesis holds my gaze for a moment, letting her words sink in.

"Are you saying what I think you're saying?" I ask.

"If you go back far enough, say, taking on the sins of

Warren and Abigail, what do you think might happen?" she says, taking a step back to give me space to consider.

I tug my eyebrows in, confused. "That would break the family curse. Abigail would be free to cross over."

"Ah, well, yes. But it's more significant than that," she says raising a finger. "Ordinarily, you wouldn't be able to consume the sins of a lost relative. Once they've left for the afterlife, your chance is lost. However, when a remnant exists..." Lachesis pauses, cocking her head slightly, "such as Abigail. Should you consume the sins keeping her in this realm, the act erases those sins completely. As in, it wipes them from existence."

"Okay?" I say, not quite following her train of logic.

She shrugs. "Granted, they would still be etched into your soul—and that's something you'll have to be judged for at the time of *your* death. But it would spare your child."

"So, let me get this straight... All I have to do is start my sin-eating with Abigail?"

"Yes." She nods.

"What's the catch?" I say, shaking my head. "That seems way too convenient. Am I sent to hell or something?"

Lachesis scrunches her face. "Well, where you would be sent to after judgement is hard to say. I cannot be certain. I'm not the one at the scales. However, what I do know is this... Should you accept the sins of Abigail—the act erases everything. The curse, your family's history with the curse..." She clasps her hands together, intertwining her fingers. Slowly, she raises both index fingers and presses them against her lips. She watches me closely, but continues. "This also means you, poor Wade here, and *your child* would be free of the curse. Debts paid in full, and all that."

"Well, that's all I need to know, then. Where do I sign up?" I say, breathing a sigh of relief. If there's a way to save them all—what more do I need? Of course, I'll take it.

Her face darkens and she eyes me from under her brows. "An act such as this *alters time*, Autumn. Accepting the sins upon yourself erases them from history. I'm not sure you're understanding the gravity of this. It could be that your family makes different decisions. Your life may take a different path. Maybe at the end of things, you never meet Wade, never fall in love..." She bites her lip. "Never have a child together."

"What?" I blurt, my voice trembling. She's right, I wasn't understanding the gravity at all. Not even a little bit.

"This is the only way," Lachesis says, placing a hand on my shoulder.

I shrug away from her touch and back away. "No—no, no. That can't be the only way."

I'd do anything to help those I love. But this?

How do I choose between freeing everyone from the burden of this curse...when the cost is possibly erasing my relationship with Wade—and even *the life of our child?*

CHAPTER 21
PULLING THE STRINGS

I can't help but wonder... Has Fate been pulling the strings all along?

Here I thought I might have had the upper hand, even if it was only for a brief moment. Dominic seemed to think forcing me into the realm of the dead was the only way to make a move without the Fates overhearing, yet here we are. Two of the three were more than well-informed.

They're actually cheering me on.

"Look, kiddo, I know this isn't the choice you wanted, but it's the one before you. Regardless, if you're going to make a move, whatever it is, it needs to be soon. Aisa's been given her instructions and she'll be coming for you both soon enough," Lachesis says, pressing her lips tight.

"How do you expect me to make a decision like that? There has to be a better way," I sputter.

She shrugs, her lips sliding into somewhat of a smirk. "If you find one, I'd love to hear about it."

I scrunch my face, suddenly fully aware of who I'm

talking to. If she doesn't know whether or not a better way exists, how the hell am I going to?

"Well, my time here's up," she chuckles quietly to herself, as if she just told an inside joke. "Good luck, Autumn. I'm rooting for you."

Before I have the chance to respond, she bursts into a constellation of light particles, each twinkling until they fade out of existence before my eyes.

I stare at the spot where she stood until my legs give out and I drop to the floor, kneeling beside Wade's bed.

What do I do? If I follow the advice of Lachesis, am I playing right into their hands? Could it be a scheme to perpetuate this curse? Then again, what if it's not? What if this really is the only way to make things work?

Being a sin-eater doesn't sound ideal—hell, it sounds downright awful when I think about it. But if it means protecting those around me, I'd damn myself to a thousand hells.

Besides, if I don't, what would it mean for Wade? For myself...our child?

We're already backed into a corner.

There's no telling if Lachesis was telling the truth about Wade's mark. If she's right and the mark was to somehow hide him from the Fates, why would his father lie to us? Does that mean Wade could still become an Angel of Death? Or will he be punished for trying to fly under their radar?

Even if the Fates let me live long enough to give birth —and I highly doubt that—our child will be cursed just like I am. It will never end until someone puts a stop to it. Or until the Blackwoods die out completely, regardless of what other families might be entangled in the web, too.

No, there really *isn't* a choice.

I have to do whatever I can to end the curse for us all before I run out of options. If it means trusting Lachesis's advice, then so be it.

A fresh sense of nausea rolls through me. I swallow hard, unsure whether it's morning sickness or nerves. Either way, it's my body's response to the decision formulating and becoming more concrete. I wish things were different. I wish I had been able to tell Wade about this pregnancy and we could have talked about it. He would have been so excited—of that, I have no doubt.

As it stands, he might never even know.

I lift my forehead from the bed rail and look up at his resting face. For the moment, he looks so peaceful, but the inky black tendrils have managed to snake their way up to his neck. Dark-purple streaks have interwoven themselves with the black, giving off a strange air of oppression.

Pushing up to a stand, I run my fingertips along the tendrils. "What should I do, Wade?" I whisper.

I know what he'd tell me. He'd tell me to find another way. He'd tell me trusting the Fates—hell, trusting Dominic—was naive.

We'd be researching sin-eaters, the lore and history, and most likely, searching for another way to make this work. But we'd end up at the same conclusion. If my father spent his whole life looking for a loophole and came up short, how can I be expected to find the answer in a few short months?

Exhaustion threatens to pull me under and my thoughts turn into a foggy mess.

Running my fingertips from Wade's collar bone to his lips, I sigh. Maybe I should just rest on this and see what I think then. It's been a long, depleting day. Maybe some sleep, even for a little bit, would help me to clear my head.

I look around the room, but none of the chairs look entirely comfortable. My gaze shifts back to Wade and a fresh wave of despair crashes over me. If this is my last night with him, I won't spend it apart.

Without another thought, I carefully move all of the wires and tubes over to the left side of the bed and crawl in beside Wade. I inch closer, resting my head on his chest and wrapping my right arm around his torso. For the longest of moments, I lay there, listening to the sound of his shallow breathing and the palpitations of his heart. Even with all that's gone on with him, I can still feel him here with me. He's still attached to his body, still fighting to return.

Closing my eyes, I settle into the loaded moment, trying to pretend I can't hear the beeping of the machines or the sounds of people in the hallway. Darkness comes for me, claiming my thoughts and I let it tug me under.

I don't know how long I slept, but I'm startled awake by the sounds of alarms. Blinking the away the confusion and disorientation, it takes me a moment to realize where I am and what's actually going on.

Nurses pour into the room, with Dr. Lockstad close behind. Her hair is pulled into a braid—different from the last time I saw her.

"You shouldn't be resting here," a male nurse says, extending a hand to help me off the bed.

"I—I know," I say, trying to get my faculties back online.

"I'm sorry, you'll need to step outside, Ms. Blackwood," Dr Lockstad says, sweeping her arm toward the door.

Unlike before, there's an edge of panic that makes my stomach lurch.

"Is he—? He's going to be okay, right?" I sputter, looking back at Wade and then to the monitors as I try to make sense out of what's going on.

Dr. Lockstad eyes the male nurse. "Can you get her out of here?"

Without a single word, he walks over to me and presses a firm hand to my back. He ushers me toward the door. "Please go down to the waiting area. We'll come get you as soon as we can." His voice is far more even-keeled than the doctor's, but still does nothing to quell the panic rising inside of me.

I shake my head, my voice reaching a far higher octave than anticipated. "No, I won't leave him." I dig my heels in, refusing to leave the room.

Without warning, a black cloud unfolds in the middle of the room. It starts small and expands outward until Wade's dad walks out.

At first, I'm almost relieved to see him, until I realize what it could actually mean.

"No, no..." I say, shaking my head in warning to him.

"Goddamn it. Even when I know this is a supernatural case, I never expect stuff like this to actually happen in my hospital," Dr. Lockstad says, pressing her fingertips to her chest and exhaling slowly.

"This is Wade's dad," I say, my voice rising to a higher octave.

"I don't care who he is," she spits back. "Please—the two of you need to step into the hall. We need to work here."

Wade's father turns his piercing stare to her. His silver

gaze floats up and down her length, as if sussing out whether or not it's worth fighting her or not. Instead, his gaze moves past her and rests on Wade. For a moment, his features soften.

"Very well," he says. Without another word, he walks out into the hallway.

I stand in the middle of the room with my mouth hanging open. But after a moment, I follow him, afraid to be left alone in the room with all the commotion.

"You can't take him," I say, jutting out my chin in defiance.

But deep down, even before he says a word, I know if he's here to take Wade, there's nothing I can do to stop him.

People in the hallway stop to stare at us, but I can't even bring myself to care.

"You know as well as I do, it's his time," the Angel of Death says, his voice nothing more than a hint above a whisper.

"I don't understand. Why can't you do something? Stop this—" I plead, pointing back to Wade's room. "It's too early. He's too young."

"You know very well my powers are limited," he says, a hint of sadness hidden in his tone. "As much as I'd like to change his course, I still have to bend to the direction things have been taken."

"What about the mark? What's going to happen to him if he—" the word gets stuck in my throat and I fight the urge to be sick.

Even after all the death I've seen, this is one I can't accept.

He straightens his shoulders, but doesn't say anything at first.

"You lied to us about what it was," I say, clenching my fists.

His lips are a thin line, but he nods. "It was for your own protection. If you were to know what it truly was, I was afraid it would do more harm than good."

A peculiar sense of relief washes over me. "So, he's not expelled?"

The Angel of Death eyes me silently for a moment. "No."

Solace mixes with anger. All this time, we thought he no longer had the legacy of powers. That he was mortal, but in just as much danger as I am. And while that might be true, he's actually safe. He might die, yes. But he'll come back. He just won't be human. He'll be forced to do his work as—

"I'm pregnant. Did you know that?" I blurt out. "If I can survive this—our child will be without a father. You know what that did to Wade. How can you allow this to happen?"

My phone starts ringing in my pocket, but I don't dare remove my glare from Wade's father to check it.

The Angel of Death's eyes flash with a mixture of hurt and anger and he steps forward, suddenly looming over me. "I have done nothing but try to protect the two of you. Much to the detriment of my own safety—as well as his, I might add. If I interfere any more, the results would be far more catastrophic."

"More catastrophic? Is that meant to be funny?"

"Child, your pitiful human existence is a blip on the map of the universal flow. What do you think would happen if the Angel of Death's lineage were to be cursed the way your family has been?"

I take a step back, considering his words. "I...I don't know," I admit.

"It would be the start of annihilation," he says, his nostrils flaring.

"Why do you think I tried so hard to keep you two apart?" he says, his forehead a cluster of contempt. "I don't want him to miss out on his family the way I did. But there were signs—far before you and Wade ever met. The signs all pointed to two possibilities. Wade's early death or the end of the delicate balance of existence. I thought if I could just keep the two of you apart..."

All of a sudden, a loud, persistent alarm sounds from Wade's room. I turn, horrified by the screech of it because I know exactly what it means.

Wade's heart is flatlining.

CHAPTER 22
THE ONLY WAY FORWARD

I turn to the doorway, my heart in my throat.

The monitors continue to squeal their death cry and Dr. Lockstad rushes back and forth in a flurry of activity. Both nurses flit around like bats, hitting different locations in the room and handing things to her as she barks out orders.

"No, no—it's too soon. I'm not ready," I squeal, spinning back to Wade's dad. "Do something. Stop this."

His face hardens, but he doesn't make a single move.

"Goddamn it," I spit. "You're the Angel of Death, for fucksake. You're telling me you're just gonna sit this one out?" Twisting on my heel, I plan to rush straight into the room and do whatever I can.

To hell with the rules.

I'd damn myself and everyone in this whole godforsaken world to have him safe and sound.

Instead, I'm pulled up short as Wade's dad grabs hold of my wrist. "I know what you're thinking, but you can't go in there. You'll do more harm than good. Trust me. You have a bigger role to play than that." His silver eyes bore through me, breaking my heart a little bit more.

"But—"

Suddenly, my phone goes off again, making me jump. This time, I pull myself out of the Angel of Death's grip and yank it from my pocket.

I press the answer button without even looking at who's calling.

"What the fuck did you do?" Diana Hawthorne says, not lending to any pleasantries.

My mouth falls open and for the briefest of moments, I'm pulled from my utter anguish to be completely confused.

"What do you mean?" I say, shaking my head. "I didn't *do* anything."

"Yeah, well, the universe begs to differ," she laments. "You've pissed off some seriously big players."

I exhale, dropping my gaze to the tiles, and running my fingertips along my forehead. "Tell me something I don't know. Do you have anything useful?"

"Well, I could have warned you, if you would have answered your damn phone," she laments. "We're on our way, but you need to do some serious backpedaling. Where are you? Who are you with?"

"I'm at the hospital with Wade. He's—" my voice cracks and I can't bring myself to say the rest. Instead, my eyes dart to his bed as the medical personal continue to do their best to bring him back.

"Things are shifting too fast for me to get a clear read. Whatever is going on, it sent me into a brain-splitting, migraine-inducing vision that yanked me straight out of a dead sleep. The world's about to go supernova and from best I can tell, you're at the epicenter," Diana says, her words spewing out hard and fast.

"Don't be ridiculous," I say, looking over my shoulder at Wade's dad.

The Angel of Death's eyes are focused into the hospital room, but a new look of apprehension has replaced his previous reserve.

"What is it?" I say, twisting back to the room with the phone still clutched to my ear.

The nurses and doctors take a step back, their faces grim.

"I'm going to call it," Dr. Lockstad says, looking at her wrist. "Time of death, 1:43 a.m."

My knees give out and I fall forward, landing hard on the tiled floor. "No..."

"You have to let me do my job," the Angel of Death says, stepping past me. His hand brushes the back of my head as he moves into place.

I shake my head, unable to accept what I'm seeing. This can't be real. It can't be happening...

Not *Wade*.

"Autumn—Autumn are you still there?" A tiny voice calls out from the phone still clutched in my hand.

Slowly, I lift it to my ear.

"He's dead," I whisper, blinking back tears. There's nothing else Diana could possibly say that would matter more than that.

I press the red button, unable to stop the numbness that attacks me outright.

After all the death I've witnessed these past few years, this has the ability to hollow me completely. Not even the loss of my father did that.

Dr. Lockstad turns to face us, her expression full of empathy. "I'm so sorry. We did everything we could."

The two nurses continue to flit around the room, but I can't bring myself to care about anything they do. I can only stare at Wade's lifeless form as I fight back the nausea rolling through me.

Suddenly, something in the energy of the room shifts.

I didn't notice the light particles that spread throughout Wade's body until his spirit, soul—whatever you want to call it—pulls back from the cells in his human shell. It melds together, congealing into a bright silver ball just above his abdomen. A thin silver string, just like the one I followed in the realm of the dead, materializes from the orb, revealing itself as connected to the Angel of Death.

Wade's dad lifts his chin slightly and his shoulders noticeably relax.

Despite myself, I push to a stand. My legs feel like they could give out at any moment, but I edge forward, holding onto the doorway for support.

Everything inside me screams to do something —*anything*. Bring him back, make him whole again. Defy the Fates and tell them where to shove it.

But the numbness consumes me, blanking out the desire to even breathe.

I'm so done.

Let them come for me. They can take me, for all I care.

"Welcome home, my son," the Angel of Death says, his arms out wide, as if he plans to hug the orb.

The doctor shoots him a strange look, then catches the attention of the nurses. Without a word, she tips her head toward the door and the three of them make a quick exit, clearly unsure what to think.

I step back, allowing them to pass by. They each say something to me as they squeeze past, but I can't seem to make any of it out. I just nod, staring at the angel in the room and the bright silver orb as it shifts, re-materializing into a human shape before my eyes.

The room fills with an intense energy—like every emotion wrapped up into one is somehow able to flood into the tiny ten-by-ten-foot space.

Before I know it, the silver orb transforms completely, taking a perfect resemblance of Wade's previous form, despite the fact that his physical body is getting cold on the bed behind them.

Another bout of nausea rolls through me, and I cover my mouth to fight back the urge to vomit.

The silver light diminishes as the form is complete, and yet there's a faint, glowing orb of energy that pulsates around the two of them.

"Hello, Wade," his father says, smiling softly.

Wade smiles back, looking happier than I've seen him in a long time. "Dad. Why are you here? What's—" he pivots slightly to the side, stopping when he sees his body on the hospital bed. Twisting around, he takes in more of the room, his eyes wild and brows tugged in. Again, he stops when he sees me in the doorway. "Autumn?" he says, his voice barely a whisper.

Tears flood my eyes and I can't hold back the torrent as they release. A garbled cry escapes my lips, but I can't find the words. Nothing I say will make any of this right.

Wade leaves his dad behind, moving quickly to my

side. "Don't cry, Autumn. Don't——" he whispers, trying to console me.

"I couldn't save you. I couldn't..." My voice catches at the back of my throat and I press my fingertips to my mouth. My gaze drops to the floor because looking at him now makes my heart feel like it's going to shatter into a million pieces. He's here—but not.

"Shhhh... It's okay. It's not your fault," he says, reaching out and placing his hands on either side of me. No longer warm, his touch is like a cool breeze, making the hairs on my arm stand on end. "Maybe this was just..."

I look up, large tears dropping my from my lower lids and onto my cheeks. "Don't you dare say it."

"*Fate.*" The word tumbles out before he has the chance to take it back.

My face crumples and my shoulders cave. Wade pulls me into him, wrapping his arms around my shoulders and pressing me to his chest. The intense chill ripples through me, but I lean into it, wishing it would just wash me away.

"I'm still here," he whispers, running his hand over the back of my head.

"No, you're not. You'll leave me. The way your dad left you. I'll be all alone——"

"No, you won't. You'll have our *child*," he says, pulling back and staring me straight in the eye. His right hand floats down, pressing against my abdomen.

My breath catches. He knows about the pregnancy.

"It's not the same," I whimper, wiping back the tears as they spill across my cheeks.

He sighs heavily. "I know. I know it's not. But it's the best I can do."

"I don't want to live in a world without you in it. It's

not fair," I say, my chin quivering and every fiber of my being screaming in agony.

Wade's father approaches us, lifting his left hand to place it on Wade's shoulder. "We need to go. I know you don't want to, but your initiation must begin to solidify your role as an Angel of Death," he says softly.

"I don't want to leave her. Not like this," Wade says, tears clouding his own eyes.

"When that is over, you can come back for longer periods of time," his father offers. "But for now, we must get your initiation underway or your soul will be swept up into the realm of the dead. Let's try and avoid that, okay?"

Wade nods faintly. "All right." He turns back to me, placing his hands on either side of my face and making me look directly into his silver eyes. "I'll be back as soon as I can. I promise you."

"But it isn't forever—" I sob.

His lower lip tugs downward, making his chin compress. "It's always forever."

With that, his lips crush down on mine, sending a chill through me that reaches all the way to the tips of my fingers and toes. I reach up, entwining my fingers in his hair, only half aware of the fact that it's not his real hair—or his real body I'm kissing.

After a moment, he pulls back, resting his forehead against mine. "I know this isn't what we wanted. But it's the only way forward."

"I know," I mutter, closing my eyes to fight back the emotions threatening to devour me whole.

But no matter what I try, my world is spinning seriously out of control.

Wade moves abruptly, kissing me on the cheek and

turning back around to face his dad. "All right. I guess I'm ready as I'll ever be." He gives my hand one last squeeze as he steps away from me.

"Sorry, dear. But you're not going to get off quite so easily," a woman's voice says.

Materializing out of the shadows in the room, an older woman clad in a dark woolen cloak appears just to the left of Wade. Before we have time to react, she reveals an enormous pair of shears from under her cloak. Then, within seconds, she severs the silver cord of light binding Wade to his father.

"No—" the Angel of Death cries out, lunging forward.

But it's too late. The silver string and the strong aura that flowed around the two of them dissipates, leaving Wade in a hazy gray cloud.

Aisa twists around, squaring off with Wade's father. "How dare you try to defy us? You know his role in all of this, just as well as I. You will not be allowed to circumvent it."

Without warning, Wade's soul is thrust back into his body. For the briefest of moments, euphoria takes me over as he sits up, clutching at his chest and coughing life back into his lungs.

However, the mark on his chest detonates in a flurry of red and gold flames until there's not a single trace left of it. Then the inky black lines that had spun themselves outward from the mark on his chest erupt, consuming every square inch of his skin. His silver eyes darken until even the whites are crowded out by the darkness.

"What the hell?" I screech, rushing into the room.

Before I can reach him, both his father and I are thrust backward as Aisa raises a single hand in our direction. I fight against whatever energetic hold she has on us, but it's no use.

Aisa's smile widens into a lopsided smirk, and without even looking at Wade, she says, "It's time to ride, *Horseman*. You have work to do."

My heart skips a beat, lodging itself firmly in my throat.

Horseman?

As in...one of the Four Horsemen of the *Apocalypse?*

Oh, my god. This can't be happening.

CHAPTER 23
FAIL-SAFE

As if everything that happens next is up to free will, Aisa chuckles to herself and vanishes in the same swirl of sparks that Lachesis did.

Her laughter rings in my ears as Wade's dad and I drop to the floor, landing hard on our feet and crumpling to the tiles. However, the Angel of Death is faster than I am. He's on his feet and rushing over to Wade before I've even managed to collect my bearings.

Wade's blackened form leaps from the bed, ripping off the hospital gown and dropping it to the floor. A strange, guttural sound escapes his lips as the bones inside him begin to snap and bend, growing in both height and size.

Stepping out in front of Wade's deforming body, the Angel of Death stretches his arms out wide. "Wade, you have to fight this. Don't let the Moirai win."

However, what stares back at him is undoubtably no longer Wade. Instead, the Horseman tilts his head down, his black eyes staring straight through the Angel of Death.

"Wade, *please*," his father pleads. It's a last feeble attempt—even I know that.

The Horseman responds with a quick, forceful jab through the Angel's abdomen. His black fist protrudes through the other side for a moment, then disappears when he retracts it.

The Angel of Death collapses, falling in some sort of bizarre slow motion.

"No—" I cry out, crawling my way to him and yanking him backward as quickly as I can.

His breathing is labored as he struggles to hold himself together. "Use...the...box," he says softly as something akin to black blood oozes from his lips. He reaches out, clutching my hands in his. His eyes plead with me but dim all too quickly.

Slumping forward, his body disintegrates into a cloud of black smoke that disperses right through my outstretched hands.

Before I can stop myself, I scream. The sound does nothing to deter the Horseman as he turns his horrifying black stare toward me. Instantly, I know there's no way I can outrun him, and he's clearly got no qualms about killing people who are in his way. Even ones his body would have otherwise cared about.

Without a second thought, I propel myself from my physical body, forcing myself into astral form in the hopes that it might confuse the Horseman long enough for me to regroup. My body drops, and for a moment, the Horseman halts his progress forward.

If this form could breathe, I'd be holding my breath, hoping he doesn't realize my heart is still beating.

When my body doesn't move, the Horseman drops to

CARISSA ANDREWS

his hands and knees, prowling forward like some kind of feral animal. Even in this form, I can feel the energy of the room shift as the Horseman bends closer to my body. His tongue flicks outward as he tests the air.

"Come out, come out," he chides, his voice a deep baritone that sends a chill straight through me.

I don't take the bait. But I also don't leave. If there's one thing I know, it's that I need to get my ass out of here and find a way to warn everyone. I can't do that if I'm dead, and I sure as hell can't do that in this form.

"Hey, you big black oaf. What do you think you're doing? Leave the girl alone," Diana Hawthorne calls out from the doorway. Behind her, Cat and Colton look like they're ready for the beat-down of the century.

When the Horseman of Death looks over his shoulder, Diana juts her chin out, blowing some stray pink hairs out of her face.

"If you really want a challenge, how about picking on someone who *can't* die," she says, placing a hand on her hip.

The Horseman turns, clearly more interested in this new prey than the measly little girl crumpled on the floor. He rises, his black body almost tall enough to reach the ceiling.

"Ooooh, shit. Here he comes," Diana mutters, her blue eyes wide as she spins on her heel.

The three of them race off down the hall and the Horseman takes the bait and rushes out the door after them.

Relief floods through me and I don't hesitate. I drop back into my physical form, with the clear intention of getting as far away from here as I can. There's no time for fear or grief. I need to get somewhere safe and figure out my next move.

As I regain my physical bearings, I scramble to my feet. In the distance, I can hear the commotion caused in the wake of the Horseman and his chase. Screams pierce the silence and some are abruptly cut off in mid-tone.

My stomach rolls and I find myself again fighting the urge to be sick. Holding onto my stomach, I race from the hospital room, running the opposite direction from where Diana and the others ran. I need to put as much distance as possible between us.

Turning the corner, I slam straight into my mom. I let out a surprised squeal, collapsing into her.

"What in the hell is going on?" she asks, craning around me to get a better view.

"Everything—" I wail. "Oh, my god, Mom. Wade..." Tears rush to my eyes and for a moment, she tugs me into her.

"I'm so sorry, honey," she whispers.

"Mom, it's not safe. We can't stay here," I say, breaking the connection. I know what she thinks has happened, and while she's partially right, I don't want her to witness the rest of it.

"What do you mean? What's happened?" she asks, alarm rising in her tone.

I try to catch my breath and force my mind to form the words. "Wade—the Moirai—"

"Slow down. Tell me what happened," Mom says, holding onto my upper arms and steadying me.

Swallowing hard, I say, "Aisa's cursed Wade. He's become a Horseman." The last word squeaks out of my mouth and I cover my lips with the back of my hand. "We have to run. He's already killed his father."

My mom's eyes widen and she breathes, "An Angel of Death has been killed?"

I nod frantically.

"Holy shit," she says, raising her fingertips to her mouth. "This is bad. Very, very bad. You're right, we need to get out of here."

In total agreement, I turn to run the way she had come, but Mom yanks me back. "Wait, wait. Do you have your backpack?"

"Forget the damn backpack," I cry, waving a hand dismissively.

"No, we need to go back and get it. I know what the writing on the box means," Mom says, clutching my arm.

"What?" I ask, unable to fight the panic telling me to run. Run like hell and never look back.

Mom exhales, her eyes closing for a moment in concentration. "It says, 'Gift to the ones with the power to wield it. Prison for the sins that lay waste.' Autumn, do you have any idea what this means?" Mom asks, her hazel eyes flashing.

"Not in the least," I mutter, wishing it made even a semblance of sense right now.

Her eyebrows tug in and her jaw sets. "Autumn, I think you were somehow gifted Pandora's Box."

I shake my head and back away. "That can't be right."

"Of course it can be. The box was lost in antiquity, but somehow it's made its way to you. There has to be a reason for it. Some way we can use it to our advantage," she says, her words coming out in an urgent whisper.

"I have absolutely no..."

Suddenly, everything is all too clear. Sin-eating, the box, the end to the curse. All of it.

For the first time in forever, hope floods my being and I look back into my mother's confused eyes. "I know what I need to do," I say, my mouth dropping open.

"What is it?" she asks.

A high-pitched scream erupts down the hall, making us both jump. It's closer than before.

"There's not enough time. You're right, I need to go back for the box," I say. "But I'll have to do everything from the room. "

"Let's go. Whatever you need, I'm with you," Mom say, reaching for my hand and giving it a squeeze. "I tried keeping you from this life. But I'll be damned if I'm going to let it take you from me without a fight."

I tip my head, stepping forward and wrapping my arms around her neck. "Thank you."

"I love you, sweetheart. Now, let's put an end to the apocalypse."

Together, we rush back to Wade's room. There's a trail of blood and scattered body parts at the far end of the hallway, and it takes everything I have to walk back into the place where all of the devastation started.

"I'll stand guard," Mom says, sliding into the room and closing the door behind us. "But whatever you're planning, do it fast." She mutters something under her breath and the seams of the door light up in a bright light that etches itself into the creases.

Scrambling to the other side of the room, I dive to the floor and pull my backpack close to me. I can't believe all this time I held onto something so powerful and it was just sitting in my backpack.

I wrench the bag open and pull out the small wooden box, staring at it with a completely different perspective. If my mom is right, if this is the box that inspired Pandora's myths, then maybe...just maybe I can do something to set things right.

"What are you going to do?" Mom asks, turning to look at me.

I glance up, settling into a strange sense of calm. "You'll see. No time to explain."

Her forehead wrinkles, but she nods.

Outside, another scream makes us both jump. "He's coming, Autumn. If he senses either of us in here—"

The door suddenly throbs with the force of an explosion, but somehow manages to stay on its hinges.

Mom stumbles back, her arms raised in front of her. "Hurry!" she yells, her eyes wide as she turns back to the door. She splays her fingers wide as she mutters words I have never heard before. Bright light emanates from her palms, intensifying the light binding the door.

My heart thumps against my ribcage, and all I can think about is how this is the only thing that makes any sense. If it doesn't work—nothing else will. This will be the end of the line.

I flare my nostrils and inhale deeply. "All right, Autumn. I sure as hell hope you know what you're doing," I mutter to myself, turning my gaze to the small wooden object in my hands.

Closing my eyes, I focus on the box with the extrasensory sight Abigail had me work on. In my mind's eye, a pattern emerges on the outside of the box. The bright, neon-like light moves almost slowly, edging from piece to piece. A sense of relief swells, but I don't have time to give in to it. This might still blow up in my face if I'm not careful.

There's no way I'm about to do as Lachesis suggested. It might make sense to her, but even if I trusted her, it's not enough.

Releasing Abigail and Warren's sins won't stop something like this from happening again to Wade. Even in another timeline, even in another life, he could be called forth as a Horseman. There could always be another reason.

His father knew this was coming. He knew how big this was about to become and how devastating it would truly be. There were so many ways he tried to stop it from coming to pass, but he had one fail-safe.

This box.

There's no way he entrusted me with Pandora's Box, a box that can trap sins and the evil of this world, simply to save my own family.

No, it's much, much bigger than that—and I intend to see it through.

Settling into the energy of the box, my fingertips work swiftly to unlock the wooden puzzle. As it begins to open, one small wooden component at a time, the gravity of this situation consumes me.

This is what I was made for. Understanding the delicate balance of life and death...knowing how important it is to wield the power wisely was only the beginning. It brought me into alignment with my ultimate destiny—to put an end to fate itself.

I need to consume the *sins of the Moirai.*

CHAPTER 24
THE BOX

The vibration in the air reaches a fever pitch as the box gets closer to opening fully. The power of the box is evident, and even if it's not Pandora's Box, whatever it is, it has the ability to cause some serious damage. Each piece slides back and forth, operating in tandem like a wooden Rubik's Cube.

For a moment, the pounding on the other side of the door ceases and shouts erupt in the hallway. I look up just in time to see the Horseman lifted off of his feet and flung away from the tiny hospital door window. Tiles, boards, and steel beams follow after him and instinctively, I know this is the work of Colton and his abilities. At this moment, I couldn't be more grateful to have him here. I just hope I have it in me to make their efforts and any sacrifices worth it.

Diana yells something, but I can't make out her words over the sounds of crunching metal and debris. Shuddering away the images it conjures, I take a deep breath and turn back to the box.

My vision shows me the final three moves and I continue quickly until I remove the final piece. The top of the box opens like a time-lapse video of a flower opening. Bright-white light spews from the opening, making me shield my eyes with the back of my right hand.

Mom twists around, shielding her eyes as well.

The lights in the room dim, then flicker off as the box creates a sort of energy vacuum. The hairs all over my body stand on end, but I can't seem to tear my eyes away from the white light. It's as if I could just crawl into it and stay there forever.

Maybe I should just...

"Close the box," Mom yells, dropping her arms, and racing toward me. "You can't have it open until you're ready. It's too dangerous."

She reaches forward, pressing her hands to the top components, and forcing them closed one by one. As the last piece locks down, the light instantly goes out, plunging us into semi-darkness. It only lasts a moment because emergency lighting suddenly floods into the room, casting a strange orange-and-red glow.

"That was close. Thank you," I mutter, shaking my head. "I don't know what came over me. I couldn't look away from the light."

"Its magick resonates with you. You'll need to be more careful," Mom says, pulling her shaking extremities back from the box. Her hands are charred black as the skin burns from her fingertips to her forearms.

"Mom," I gasp, nearly dropping the box. "*Your hands.*"

She returns her determined gaze to me and holds out a burnt palm between us. "Forget it. They will heal. Focus on your mission. There's a homicidal Horseman on the loose and we don't want to be on the receiving end of whatever he has in mind. Trust me."

My mouth snaps shut, and I nod. She's right. Besides, if this goes the way I think it will, none of this will matter. What I'm about to do could alter everything.

Swallowing hard, I soften my focus on her hands and look past them to the commotion in the hallway. I can make out Diana and Cat, but Colton must be somewhere near the Horseman. Blood is smattered against the side of Diana's face, but her expression is as fierce as ever.

I can't believe any of this. It's like a nightmare beyond anything I could have imagined. Wade's gone and his body has become a Horseman for the end of days.

The box is in my periphery, reminding me of everything that needs to happen and why.

Turning back to Mom, I fight back angry tears and say, "I might need your help for what comes next. We need to get the Fates here."

"The Moirai?" she says, clearly startled. "Why?"

"Because I'm taking them down," I say, my jaw firm. "It's the only way this ends. I think that's what Wade's father wanted me to do. I think this box is meant to trap *their* sins—their discretions. But it's too big for me to do it alone, so it needed to be housed somewhere else."

Her eyes are wide, hazel orbs. "Are you sure?"

"Not really, but I have to try," I say. "Can you help me? I don't know if I can do it alone."

Dropping to her knees beside me, she nods. "If you want to summon the Moirai, it requires a lot of power. But the Moirai are bound by the laws of the Ancients. In many ways, they're more susceptible to the pull of magick than even you and I are. If we summon them forth with clear intention, they should be forced to heed our call."

All of a sudden, the commotion on the other side of the hospital room door kicks up again. By the looks of it, the Horseman has managed to break free from whatever Colton and the others were doing. Colton's form flies through the air and the backlash from this turn of events is a fireball so big it unleashes the hospital's sprinkler system.

Water pours out of the little ceiling spigots, dousing everything.

"Goddamn it, Cat—" Diana curses from somewhere nearby.

The Horseman laughs, and the deep, jovial nature of it sends a shiver straight through me. Suddenly, his black streak rushes past the window and without a shadow of a doubt, I know Diana and the others are in serious trouble.

My heart leaps into my throat and I know it's now or never.

"Come on, Moirai. Is this all you've got?" I yell, directing my anger and terror in their direction. Water cascades in sheets across my face, and I wipe it away with the back of my hand. "Why don't you come back here and be a part of this fight? Or are you the type that only lets others do your dirty work? I bet that's it, right?"

"You need to use their names," Mom warns, cradling her hands to her torso. Water drips from the ends of her hair, but she doesn't even shudder.

I set down the box in front of me and tip my chin in acknowledgment. Then, I tip my gaze to the ceiling, as if they are somehow watching me from above the way a scientist watches rats trapped in a maze.

"Clotho, Lachesis, Aisa—where are you? Come out and join this mess you've created," I demand, balling my fists at my side. "You wanted this. Come get your own hands dirty."

"Speaking of hands, hold mine. You're right, you need help. The message will broadcast better if we summon them together. They won't be able to ignore the both of us," Mom says, extending her charred hands. The blackened skin is already flaking away, dropping to the floor in large chunks as the water hits it. Bones peek out from underneath, their soft white in clear contrast to the dying skin.

"What about—" I say, pointing.

"It's fine. We need to make a physical connection through our energetic centers. The hands are secondary chakras. This is the easiest way," she says, flicking her skeletal fingertips.

I shoot her an apprehensive look.

"It's only pain, Autumn. I'll live," she reiterates.

Cat screams in the hallway. It's the kind of blood-curdling scream that comes from true pain.

Pressing my lips tight, I reach out, grabbing hold of her hands as lightly as I can, given the panic rising inside me.

She winces slightly and lets her eyes drift closed. "Here we go. Be ready," she says, nodding in my direction.

I inhale sharply. "I'm ready.

Mom exhales, trying to relax her shoulders. "Clotho, Lachesis, Aisa," she calls out. "We summon you to join us."

She doesn't wait for them to respond. Instead, she continues to repeat their names over and over again, letting the energy of it build. There's a strange vibration in the room, like too much static electricity that needs to be released soon or it could cause a spark.

I keep my eyes open wide, peering around the room as I join her. "Clotho, Lachesis, Aisa..." I call out, repeating their names like a mantra.

At first, nothing happens other than getting completely soaked by the torrent of water falling from the ceiling. Just when my insides start to scream at me, telling me this was a ridiculous idea, tiny particles of light begin to swirl around the small, enclosed space.

Within seconds, the three sisters materialize. Clotho forms fully first, her red-hooded jacket standing out in deep contrast to her sisters. She turns to Lachesis, whose white pantsuit is turning gray as the water douses it. They exchange a confused look. Aisa, on the other hand, simply flings back her black-hooded cloak, looking completely irate.

"How dare you summon us for your petty vendetta," Aisa spits, turning her wrinkled face toward us. Her bright-blue eyes flash menacingly as she takes a step toward my mother and me. "What's done cannot be undone. This is *fate*."

Lachesis and Clotho again exchange a confused glance. They edge closer together, backing away from Aisa, as if they know the tides are about to turn and their mission is to simply differentiate themselves.

"Autumn, *now*," Mom say, her voice firm, as she turns to me. Her eyebrows raise expectantly and she glances down at the box.

Letting go of her hands, I pick up the box, and fiddle with the lid to force it open again.

Aisa takes a step forward, watching my movements closely without saying a word.

The moment the box bursts open, the vacuum of light flares to life and begins to suck all energy into its center like a black hole.

Whatever power was left in the generator gives out and the sprinklers abruptly stop spewing water. The emergency lights go out with a pop and the fringes of the room drop into shadows as the box becomes the only light source.

The two younger sisters continue to stand back, but Aisa takes another step forward. For whatever reason, the box alone doesn't seem to even touch the Moirai. The three of them stand there, staring at the box with a semi-awed and confused expressions.

"Why isn't it working?" I sputter, turning to look over my shoulder at Mom.

She shakes her head frantically. "Don't look at me. I'm not the sin-eater."

Aisa raises a single gray eyebrow and nearly bursts out laughing. "And just what is it you thought would happen, child? You would trap us in the box?"

"N-no," I stutter, trying to regain my confidence. "I thought I could—"

Lachesis steps forward, leaving Clotho's side for the first time. Recognition and interest pique in her gaze. "You thought you'd consume *our* sins?"

I inhale sharply, suddenly feeling very exposed.

Aisa cackles. "You can't vanquish the sins from the *living*. You're not *God*."

Lachesis shoots me an apologetic look, but shakes her head and drops her gaze to the floor. The crease of her forehead relays the message loud and clear that she's disappointed I didn't take her advice. However, there's still a hint of something lingering in her features, but I'm not sure what it is.

My heart plummets into my stomach and I realize that I've made a terrible, horrible mistake.

"Did you put your bets on this one?" Aisa snorts, looking over at her two sisters. "You always were the fools."

Behind Aisa, the door to the hospital room thuds loudly as the Horseman tries to break the wards my mother set in place. She stands up, raising her shriveled hands to revitalize the wards, but nothing happens.

"The box must have taken some of my powers. It's not working—" she says, turning to me with terrified eyes.

Before I have time to respond, the door to the hospital room crumples inward with a force that knocks Mom and I back into the wall and window behind us. Clotho and Lachesis step back, turning to the doorway. Aisa once again cackles, clapping her hands together like a giddy schoolgirl.

"Oh no," Mom breathes, scrambling to get back to her feet.

I look up, brushing blood and debris from my face just in time to see the Horseman step into the room. From an outstretched hand, Colton dangles by his throat. Behind them, the bodies of Cat and Diana lie on the ground in a heap of blood and debris.

Oh, my god. This is how it's going to end.

CHAPTER 25
SIN-EATER

I fight back the hysteria building within me, but it's useless. Everything I know and love is coming to an end before my eyes. On top of that, everything I've been through up until now has been completely pointless. Necromancy, astral projection...even sin-eating. It's all useless.

With a sickening snap, the Horseman's black hand clenches, breaking Colton's neck and severing his head from the rest of his body. His body crumples to the floor beside the Horseman with little fanfare.

I clap a hand over my mouth, forcing back the guttural scream trying to unleash.

Immortal or not—I'm not certain anyone can survive a Horseman of the apocalypse.

Tears flood my eyes as I try my best not to give in completely to despair.

There's absolutely no resemblance to Wade remaining in the exterior body of the Horseman. It's like I'm staring at a completely different entity altogether—and in some ways, I suppose I am. Yet, I swear I can still feel him. Like he's still here with me, even though it seems impossible. God, how I wish he was still here with me.

Glancing down at the open box, I blow out a slow burst of air, trying to calm my nerves. What if there is a way to reach Wade? A way to make him remember who he really is... Even if only for a moment.

Could it be possible?

Wade never crossed over. His soul never left his body. Whatever he is now, he's some sort of distorted hybrid. Something exploited for the gains of the Moirai—or at the very least, Aisa. Maybe the universe, too. But then again, the universe rarely takes sides.

Completely ignoring the bright light and intense energy of the box still clutched in my hands, the Horseman simply flicks his wrist and Colton's head flies across the room. It hits the wall to my right with a sickening thud before it comes to a rest on the cold tile floors. Blood pools around it and I bend over, fighting back the urge to vomit.

Mom is suddenly at my side, her bony hands resting on my back as she tries her best to comfort me. It's no use though. We're all doomed.

"You know, it's ironic, really. We had no idea at first that this horrid existence was finally coming to an end," Aisa says gleefully, turning away from the Horseman to face me and my mother. "It was foretold eons before you were born, but we never knew just when the day would come. It was hidden, even from us, if you can believe it." She snickers to herself.

Lachesis turns her gaze from Aisa to me, her eyes wide. She opens her mouth, as if she's about to say something, but Clotho grabs hold of her arm. When Lachesis looks at her, Clotho shakes her head.

I narrow my gaze, unable to believe any of this.

"Why would you want to bring on the end?" I sputter, trying to stand back up.

Even as I talk to Aisa, I don't take my eyes off of the Horseman because I know he won't stand by for long. Despite myself, a plan begins to form, and a strange serenity settles over me. It may be a Hail Mary pass, but I'm ready to take it if the right moment presents itself.

"Because we'll finally be *free*," she states, as if it's the most obvious thing in the world.

My mouth drops open.

Freedom? Of all the things she wants, it's the same thing as the rest of us.

How's that for ironic?

Well, if it's freedom she wants, maybe there's more than one way to give it to her.

As if on cue, the Horseman stalks forward, his dark, hulking form sending complete terror racing through me, despite any plans. I hold out my free hand, as if my feeble hand gesture could do anything to make him stop.

"Wade—please," I plead, refusing to look away from him. "This isn't you. You don't want to do this."

"That's *not* Wade, Autumn." Mom steps closer to me, grabbing onto my right arm as she winces through the pain.

I look over my shoulder into her terrified eyes. It's clear that everything she fears about this magickal world is coming to fruition right before her and there's nothing she can do about it but watch it unfold. It must be her worst nightmare as much as it's becoming mine.

I straighten my shoulders, shaking my head at her words. "You're wrong. He's still in there...*somewhere*. I know he is. I can feel him," I say, stepping forward and pulling out of my mother's reach. My heart thumps loudly in my chest, but I can't bring myself to cower in fear anymore.

If this is going to be the end, I'm going out the way I want to—believing in the power of love. *Our love.* "Wade, if you can hear me. You can fight this. Don't be controlled by the Moirai. Don't give in to this," I say, again raising my hands out between us. "I love you."

The Horseman continues forward, making his way directly for me with determination painted across his blackened face.

"Autumn," Mom warns, her voice shaking.

It must be hard for her, being as powerful as she is and having that power weakened right when you need it most. Despite her warning, I stand my ground, refusing to back away.

"Wade, please," I beg, hoping somehow his connection to me will bring him back around.

As the Horseman reaches me, there's no sense of recognition at all. Instead, he reaches out, grabbing hold of my neck and lifting me straight off the ground.

The box drops to the floor as my hands fly to his outstretched arm out of reflex. I press my toes down, trying to touch the floor, but I barely graze it with the tip of my shoe.

Behind me, my mother scrambles to kick the box away from the Horseman's immediate reach. Then she races toward him with her hands clenched into skeletal fists. There's a strange summoning of static electricity as she nears. However, whatever power she summons has no effect on him. Without blinking or even glancing in her direction, the Horseman uses his free arm to knock her back. She sails through the air, slamming into the wall and dropping to the floor. Bits of drywall and dust crumble with her.

Instantly, the magic she had begun to call forth is extinguished. From the corner of my eye, I can see her shake her head, then slumps to the floor. I can't tell if she's okay, or if she'll try again.

It doesn't really matter, though. This is the moment I was waiting for.

My vision blurs as my throat closes under the Horseman's tight grip. Releasing my grasp on his wrist, I extend my right hand, placing it over his heart. His bare chest is cold to the touch and feels more like that of a snake than the warm place I have rested my head.

I force myself to stare deeply into the black pools of the Horseman's eyes. When I can sense a connection is made, I summon as much energy as possible to speak.

"What about our *baby*?" I say breathlessly, doing everything I can to fight against the pressure that's making the edges of my vision darken.

For the briefest of moments, the Horseman's expression shifts and a spark of recognition lights in his black eyes. It's not much, but it's enough.

"Please, remember..." I squeak.

He lowers his arm just enough for me to make contact with the ground and I take a labored inhalation. It doesn't provide the best relief, but it manages to keep the darkness at back for a moment longer.

"We're not your enemy," I say, each word more difficult

than the word before it. My hand remains on his heart and I leave it there as a reminder of our connection.

He tilts his head ever so slightly, as if pondering the meaning of my words. His grip loosens a little as he looks down at my hand, like it's the first time he noticed it was even there.

All of a sudden, he releases his hold on my neck entirely. I drop to the ground like a rag doll, unable to hold my own weight as the oxygen comes rushing back at me. Reaching up, I rub my throat, trying to get the muscles to work again.

"Enemy," the Horseman whispers.

"No," Aisa breathes, her eyes wide with shock and anger. "What are you *doing?*"

With unearthly speed—speed I didn't even realize he could wield, or I would have been absolutely immobilized by it—the Horseman turns to Aisa. Before any of the Moirai can react, he severs Aisa's head from her body and tears her dreaded shears from her hand.

As her body slumps sideways to the floor, he lunges forward, flinging the shears through the air like an expert dart player. They hit their mark, puncturing straight through the center of Clotho's chest. Blood splatters from her mouth as she turns a confused eye toward her final sister.

Lachesis reaches out, trying to catch Clotho before she falls. She barely manages to clip her sister's arm before the Horseman is behind her. She freezes, her terrified eyes searching for something...

The Horseman wraps his large black hand across the front of her face. It contrasts boldly with her pale skin as he twists her head backward with a loud snap.

Lachesis drops to the floor in slow motion, like time somehow stood still, staring in the same shock as the rest of us before time kicked back in and resumed as it should. The Horseman stands back, a sentinel for the destruction he just created.

As all three Moirai lie on the floor, the wooden box pulsates beside me and my awareness is called back to it. I pick up the box and suddenly, bright-blue light bursts from my chest, emitting a sort of force field that knocks both my mother and the Horseman back. My body rises from the floor on its own accord, hovering a few feet in the air. All I can see—all I can focus on—is the Moirai and what I now need from them. What was never meant to be theirs.

The rest of the world falls away and the only thing that exists is me...and the sins of fate.

In a sudden burst of energy, the sins rise, radiating off of the bodies of the Moirai and making their way to me. I throw my head back, my arms splayed out wide in acceptance of what is.

The sins flow to me in the form of glowing bluish smoke and I open my mouth, allowing the smoke to become a part of me. At first, memories of their transgressions are slow to come forth. It's almost as if they're somehow being clung to by the fading souls of the Moirai. Yet, one by one, their horrors flicker to life, illuminating in my mind's eye as they enter my body through any energetic means necessary. A life cut short here, a family cursed there... It was never meant to be like this.

Within this bubble of energy, their sins become one with me until I can no longer remember where I begin and they end. The effect is so intense, I close my eyes to shield myself from the magnitude of it.

Without context, some of their sins have no meaning —and perhaps they're not meant for me to understand. They're only to be consumed and locked away. Put back into the box where they can no longer harm others.

Different times and places flood past me—faster and faster until I can no longer keep up with it all. I can only hold on and hope that I'm not completely lost in it.

Once inside me, the Moirai's sins are somehow transformed into pure white light, then expelled through my hands and funneled into the box. The faster the sins come in, the faster they are transmuted and trapped inside.

All of the pressure from the Moirai's sins decreases, and my body begins to feel lighter than it has in...*forever*.

Suddenly, the box closes of its own volition as the final sin has been consumed.

The lightness doesn't last long. I double over, groping at my stomach. The force of this final moment is incredible, like I'm somehow being pulled into the gravity of a black hole.

Then everything goes a brilliant bright white as my entire existence implodes.

CHAPTER 26
MEMORIES

The energy bubble that surrounded the four of us bursts.

Nothing could have prepared me for this moment. Even if there was a way to prepare, I doubt there was ever a sin-eater who has done something like this, anyway.

As the white light pulls back, I'm left standing in the middle of an ever-shifting landscape. Days, nights, and people move all around me in rapid succession—as if the world has somehow managed to go into a super-speed rewind.

But it's more than that. All around me, even the location shifts. I go from standing in the middle of the destruction of the hospital room to an open field full of snow. Then, the courtyard of the manor, the middle of a crowded mall, a beautiful restaurant...

Even the clothes I'm wearing changes from moment to moment, shifting with the various choices that may or may not come to pass. It all depends on where I land when this crazy train stops.

The effect is dizzying, as things continue to shift around me. I close my eyes, allowing the motion and swirling sensation to roll past me and pray that it comes to an end soon.

When I open my eyes again, the location seems more settled as I stand in the middle of the sitting room at Blackwood Manor. The decor of the room changes ever so slightly, a Christmas tree in the corner by the window, then on the opposite wall. Stockings hung by the fireplace, then thick fir tree garland decorated with red bows.

What stops my heart, though, is when I see my mom walk through the manor. In one frame, she's stoking a fire, the next she's placing ornaments on the Christmas tree. In another, she's sitting on the couch and I find myself wishing for all I'm worth that whatever I did—whatever happens now—I was able to make things right with my parents, with my whole family.

The fact that I'm seeing my mom at the manor gives me hope I may have at least accomplished one good thing in all of this.

When the shift finally stops, I'm left standing beside the fireplace. My hand is outstretched, as if I was about to pick up a picture on the mantle. I continue the movement, reaching for the picture and pulling it from the shelf.

The image is of Abigail and Warren standing outside the manor. It actually reminds me of one I've seen before —but the memory is fading too quickly. There's just one difference... Rather than being young, they are both easily in their seventies and surrounded by at least twenty other people. They range in age from their fifties down to small children and babies held in arms. All of them look so incredibly happy.

"Sweetie, do you think you can help me with the place settings? Our guests should be here any minute."

I spin around, surprised and relieved to see Mom walking into the room with a tray of thick crystal glasses. She places the tray on the small drinks table beside a large punch bowl filled with what looks like egg nog.

I blink back my relief and smile. "Sure, absolutely," I breathe, grinning at her like a crazy person.

When she faces me, her eyebrows tug in and her expression turns quizzical. "Are you okay? You look a little —" she scrunches her face, "odd."

I return the picture to the mantle and rush over to her, suddenly consumed by the desire to know she's real.

"I'm fine," I murmur. Wrapping my arms around her, I pull her in tight, burying my face in the crook of her neck.

She chuckles softly, but her hands float around to my back as she embraces me in return. "What's gotten into you tonight? Did you break into the egg nog already?"

A giggle bursts from my throat. Her hair tickles the side of my cheek as I shake my head. Taking another breath, inhaling her scent, I pull away and step back.

I fight back tears as the emotions of two very separate lifetimes collide. So many of the memories from before are fading, drifting from my mind like smoke in the wind. In their place, new memories begin to take root.

"No, nothing like that. I'm just really..." Movement catches my eye and I turn to the doorway as I quietly say, "*happy.*"

"Have you seen my blue tie, dear?" Dad says, walking

to the middle of the room and fiddling with the cuff of his shirt. "I can't seem to find it anywhere."

My mouth drops open and I swear my heart stops beating.

"Dad," I breathe, racing from my mom over to the middle of the room. With the same ecstatic energy, I throw my arms around him and squeeze him tight.

"Whoa, someone's been hitting the eggnog a bit early," Dad laughs, patting me on the shoulder.

"That's what I said," Mom says, chuckling softly. "And have you tried looking in the closet?"

"The closet? Now, why would I look in there?" Dad says, his hand now resting on my shoulder as he turns to face Mom.

I exhale softly, trying to separate myself from my past memories and whatever this new present brings. Neither one of them seem aware of the momentous moment happening right now, anyway...and I'm not sure how long I'll remember it either.

Mom's here... Dad's *alive*.

I can't imagine a better outcome than that. Yet, something tugs at the back of my mind, and I can't seem to put my finger on what it is. It's on the edge of my memories, yet the more I try to focus on what it could be, the further away it slips.

The doorbell rings and Dad removes his hand from my shoulder, turning to the entryway. "Duty calls," he says, exiting the room.

"Do not use that as an excuse to forget your tie," Mom calls after him. "That man will do anything to get out of wearing a tie, I swear to god." Her words say one thing, but there's a twinkle in her eye as she walks past me and into the entryway.

Shaking away the overwhelming emotions fighting inside me, I take a deep breath and float my gaze around the room, trying to take every detail of this new reality in. The lavish Christmas decorations are something I've only seen in magazines, but they suit this room—and the manor as a whole. The white LED Christmas lights twinkle softly from just about every corner of the room, but it's the painting above the fireplace that draws my attention, now that I'm standing back.

The memories of it clash together and merge with the now. As I parse it out, I realize it's the same painting I had found in one of the abandoned rooms...

At the time, it was only of my mother—and only half done. But now, it's a finished piece and a painting of the three of us—Mom, Dad, and me.

My heart swells as I stand there, staring at it.

"There you are," Cat says in my ear as she wraps her arms around my shoulders from behind. "What are you doing in here? Ohhh, eggnog." She drops my shoulders and makes her way over to the bowl. She's dressed in a beautiful red and cream pantsuit, and it looks absolutely striking on her as she turns around with a full cup. Smiling at me, she raises the glass. "Cheers."

"Did I hear someone say eggnog?" Dominic says, walking into the room. He tips his head my direction, but heads straight to Cat.

"Dominic," I say, unable to stop myself from staring. His hair is a soft brown rather than the striking white-blond from my memories.

"That's my name, don't wear it out," he laughs, accepting a glass from Cat.

"Behave yourself, Dominic," a woman says sternly from the entryway. I turn around to see Dominic's mother, narrowing her gaze at him. "Too much alcohol isn't good for you."

I shudder away the memory as it leaves my mind, replaced by this different version of her.

She jabs her index finger in his direction and he sets the drink back down on the table, grinning at her. Appeased, she stalks out of the room, following my mom in the direction of the kitchen.

As soon as she's gone, Dominic picks up his glass, clinking it together with Cat's.

Everyone is so different... I turn back to the doorway, craning to see who else might be in the entryway.

"Where's Colton?" I ask.

"He'll be here any minute. He wanted to stop at the store to pick up some pie as a thank-you gift. Very creative, right?" Cat says, rolling her eyes. "I didn't have the heart to tell him it was probably going to be closed."

I snicker to myself, but smile.

"Come on, everyone. It's time to eat," Mom says, popping her head into the room.

"I'm starving," Dominic says, downing the rest of his glass and setting it on the drinks table. "Your mom makes the best turkey, Autumn."

Together, the three of us make our way to the dining room. Mrs. Gilbert is already seated at the table and she's leaning over, talking animatedly with Dominic's mother. Beside Mrs. Gilbert, a man who looks like an older carbon copy of Colton sits with his arms crossed and an amused grin on his face. While I had never met him before, I know instantly this is the twins' father.

"Sorry we're late, guys," Colton says, his voice carrying from the entryway.

"We?" I say, twisting around.

Beside him, Diana Hawthorn and the man named Blake are removing their coats, along with two other men. One is a little older than my friends and me, but only just. His shaggy brown hair covers part of his eyes as he flicks his head to see the rest of the room. When our eyes meet, he grins and waves.

Instinctively, I wave back, but I'm not certain if I know him or not.

The other man is flamboyantly dressed in a bright green and red suit. His hair is meticulously groomed, and I can tell instantly he's going to be a character.

Colton notices me and steps out in front. "Oh, hey, Autumn. Have you met Renaldo and Aiden?"

I shake my head, unsure what to say.

"Aiden is Blake's son, well, adopted son," Colton says, pointing to the shaggy man. "And this is Renaldo." He points to the man in the loud suit.

"Please, call me Ren," Renaldo says, stepping past Colton with a flourish and extending his hand.

I walk into the room and shake his hand. "Nice to meet you."

"Man, the snow's really coming down," Aiden says, stepping up to also shake my hand. He runs his hand through his hair, trying to dislodge it.

"Oh, honey, a little snow isn't going to hurt you. Your hair is already an injustice to haircuts everywhere," Renaldo says, tsking him under his breath.

Aiden rolls his eyes and walks past me into the dining room. Renaldo dips his chin, making a grumpy face before following after Aiden.

Colton laughs, shaking his head. "They're always like that."

"And at least you fine folks get to enjoy it for a while so I can get some peace," Diana says, making a big, Cheshire grin.

Blake nods my direction. "Good to see you again, Autumn."

I wave, still unsure how this new reality fits together. My memories are getting all muddled together and I get the distinct sense it won't get better anytime soon. Maybe after some rest...

Colton and I walk into the dining room, taking our places. I sit down toward the head of the table, beside Cat. Colton and Aiden sit on the other side of her, with Dominic, Diana, Blake, and Renaldo filing around the end of the table and up the other side.

"It's a darn good thing you have such a big table," Renaldo says, taking a seat at the end.

I nod in his direction. It's the first time I've seen so many people seated at it. In fact, it's the first time I've seen more than two of us sitting here.

Mom and Dad walk out, carrying the turkey and green bean casserole dishes. They place both in the middle of the table and take a seat opposite me.

I eye the head of the table, surprised they're planning to keep it open. However, James walks out, smiling and waving at everyone as if he's well acquainted.

"Ah, this looks delicious, Andrea," he says, patting my mom on the shoulder as he walks up. Without another word, he slides back the final chair, sitting down at the head of the table.

Confused, I narrow my gaze and flit it to my dad. He reaches out, grabbing hold of my mom's hand and giving it a squeeze. "She outdid herself this time."

"Hopefully it's as good as it looks," Mom says, a hint of rosiness creeping into her cheeks.

"I have no doubt it will be incredible. I only wish your mother were still here with us, Lyle. Christmas was always her favorite," he says, his brown eyes sparkling as he turns to my dad.

"I do, too, Dad," my father says, sighing. "But I think she's smiling down on us."

Despite myself, I double take. "Dad?"

Everyone turns to look at me with bewildered expressions.

"What's going on with you tonight, Autumn? Seriously, are you feeling okay?" Mom says, leaning across the table and placing a hand over my forehead.

James chuckles. "I know you're a big supernatural college student now, but you haven't forgotten your grandpa already, have you?"

"I, uh—" I blink hard and shake my head. "No, of course not."

As my memories try to catch up, I'm suddenly acutely aware of aspects of my life that were still hidden in plain sight before.

James is my...*grandpa?*

Mom drops back into her seat and raises her hands to the ceiling. "Okay, everybody. Dish up."

Everyone does as they're told, grabbing platefuls of food and settling back into their seats. The conversation picks up as little groups form and smaller discussions break out. The atmosphere is so lighthearted and fun, yet I still can't seem to shake this feeling like I'm forgetting something important.

I suppose it's all important. My brain is literally rewriting history inside of itself.

"So, Autumn, are you excited about the new semester?" Cat asks, nudging me. Then she leans in close and whispers, "I heard there's a few new students coming in. Maybe you'll finally find someone worthy of stealing your attention."

Suddenly my heart skips a beat and it all comes rushing back to me. A deep sorrow bubbles up and my hand instinctively drops to my abdomen.

I'm no longer pregnant, and the one person I wanted most is missing.

What's happened to Wade?

CHAPTER 27
DONE WITH FATE

As much as I try to settle into this new reality, Christmas has lost the majority of its meaning, knowing Wade is missing from my life.

For whatever reason, the memories of him refuse to fade. In all honesty, I don't know which would be worse, continuing to live without him... Or having forgotten him the way everyone else has.

Both are torture in their own right. But this way, at least I can find out if he's alive, even if he has no idea who I am.

The drive to Mistwood Point is slow and tedious, thanks to the freshly fallen snow. On the upside, it lends a mystical quality to the landscape that lifts my spirits slightly. I find myself hoping the magic in the air is a good omen.

As I get closer, my pulse begins to race. I try to think of all the things I can say to him if I see him. Or what I would ask his grandfather if he's still alive. One way or another, I will find a way to track him down.

Despite all the relief and happiness about the way things have turned out, I can't fathom not having Wade in my life. And I refuse a possible future where I don't at least try to find him.

I turn off the highway, taking the final exit that brings me to Mistwood Point. As far as I can tell, the town looks the way it did before, with some minor changes. Granted, many of my memories have faded into a dreamlike state; there are still some aspects where I can barely tell there are differences.

When I turn on the road that Wade's grandfather lived on, I have to remind myself not to grip the steering wheel so tightly. My breath becomes nothing more than shallow gulps as I pull into the driveway.

From the outside, it's hard to say if anyone is home, but one good sign is how the driveway and sidewalk have been shoveled off. Despite myself, I find myself going over the script in my head if Wade happens to answer the door.

He might be skeptical at first, but I'm fairly certain I can convince him to at least go out to dinner with me. Taking a final deep breath, I shift into park and pull the keys from the ignition. Before I can talk myself out of it, I exit the vehicle and make my way up to the front door.

My nerves are going wild, and I feel excited and jittery as I lift my hand and knock on the door. Shuffling on the front step, I pull my jacket in tighter and wait. On the other side of the door, I can hear movement as someone makes their way to answer.

Dropping my shoulders and lifting my chin, I plaster on a smile and wait.

The locks on the other side clink and the door opens. My gaze drops a foot down as I stare into the big brown eyes of a little girl who can't be more than eight years old. She blows back the bangs of her jet-black hair with a sideways puff.

"Can I help you?" she says, pulling the door in tight and eyeing me with suspicion.

My mouth is suddenly dry, but I nod and lick my lower lip. "Yes, is—is this the Hoffman residence?" I ask.

"Who is it, dear?" a woman says, walking up behind the little girl. She has the same brown eyes, but her hair is peppered with gray. Her eyebrows raise as I come into view. "Is there something I can do for you?"

"She's wondering about the Hoffman family," the little girl says.

The mother's dark eyes soften, filling with empathy as she says, "Oh, I'm so sorry to be the one to tell you this. Mr. Hoffman passed away not long ago."

My heart skips a beat and I inhale sharply. "Do you know which Hoffman? What was his first name?"

"William, I think?" the woman says, narrowing her eyes as she thinks.

I nod, relieved to hear it's not Wade. "I see. You don't happen to have a number to reach the family, do you?"

The little girl takes the moment to slip under her mother's arm and meander away. The woman takes her daughter's spot, grabbing onto the edge of the door. Shaking her head, she says, "No, I'm sorry, I don't. You could try checking with the realty company, though. We used Mistwood Point Realty. I'm sure they'd have someone on record."

Fighting back my disappointment, I attempt a smile. "Okay, thank you. I really appreciate your help."

"No problem. I wish I could have done more," she says, shooting me a quick smile and closing the door.

Turning from the door, I make my way back to my SUV and hop inside. My pulse has softened, but it still beats loudly in my ears. While I might have another lead with the realty office, they won't be open until Monday at the earliest.

So, for now, I'm no closer to finding Wade than I was before.

Putting the vehicle into reverse, I make my way to the one place where I can collect my thoughts without feeling judged. I drive into the cemetery, making my way through the large loop of the newer section and parking in front of the iron gate that marks the older section.

I park, twisting the key from the ignition. For a moment, I sit there, staring at the old headstones beyond the gate. My thoughts tussle back and forth, vying for some sort of peace I know I won't be able to find. Not even here.

Reaching over to the passenger seat, I grab my hat and tug it on my head. I leave the shelter of the SUV and make my way through the gate and into the older section, where the history rolls off of it in beautiful waves. I can feel the serenity in this place as I connect more fully to my natural gifts and the sacred space itself.

My feet crunch in the freshly fallen snow and already I can feel the tips of my toes getting cold. Yet, I can't seem to bring myself to turn around. Instead, I find myself sitting down in front of the grave of Charlotte. Her mono-lithic headstone is a testament to the beauty and care we used to put into memorial monuments.

Raising a gloved hand, I trace the decorative symbol

above her name. It almost looks like a snake eating its own tail, but the clarity of it has worn off with age, so it's hard to be sure. I stare at it, trying to place why something about it resonates within me.

"Beautiful, isn't it?" a man's voice says from behind me. I hadn't even heard him approach.

Adrenaline races through my system and I spin around, coming face to face with Wade's father.

"You," I breathe, unable to make my brain form a more intelligent sentence.

His silver eyes flash as he smiles. "And you," he says.

"You're alive?" I say, trying to process what I'm seeing.

He shakes his head, smirking. "Well, not exactly. But I exist, so there's that."

"So, you're still the Angel of Death?" I say, standing up and brushing off the snow from my jeans.

He clasps his hands in the front of his body and nods. "Indeed."

My words cling to my throat as the beat of my pulse picks up. "And Wade?"

His face darkens slightly, and he holds the crook of his arm out. "Walk with me?"

I exhale a jagged breath and loop my arm through his.

"What you did was extraordinary, Autumn," the Angel of Death says, leading me through the various headstones to the slightly less snow-covered sidewalk.

My gaze falls, and I hope he's not leading me to a headstone I don't want to see.

"I don't know about that," I say, unable to hide the worry in my voice.

"I disagree. Things are as they should be now," he says, shooting me a sideways glance.

"What does that mean?" I ask, wondering if he means that I'm no longer with Wade, like he always wanted.

He inhales slowly, his forehead creasing with thought. "You and I are the only ones who remember what things were like before. In time, it may only be me again. Your memory may fade. You are only *human*, after all." Snickering to himself, he nudges me with his shoulder.

I shoot him a knowing glance. "That's not *all* I am."

"I am aware," he says, nodding.

I sigh, letting my shoulders drop in defeat. "So, is that why you won't tell me where Wade is?" Turning to him, I watch his movements closely to see what they give away. "He's not...*gone*... Is he?"

His silver eyes practically close as he weighs what to say, and the expanding silence increases my anxiety. He continues walking, drawing out my pain.

"I can't promise how things will go from here on out. This is a future I have only experienced in theory," he says, shrugging. "This time, I have promised myself not to get involved. I will let things unfold as they will."

My anxiety eases slightly.

"Are you saying that if I were to find Wade, you aren't *necessarily* opposed to our relationship anymore?" I say, narrowing my gaze.

The Angel of Death stops walking and turns to face me. "Keeping the two of you apart was one of many attempts at keeping you on your mission."

My mouth falls open. "It was about me? I thought you said it was against—"

He raises a hand between us and tilts his head slightly. "I'm not going to say necromancers don't directly play in opposition to what angels of death are here to do. But we're not *that* inflexible."

"Unbelievable," I mutter, shaking my head and walking away.

Wade's father chuckles but follows me. "Things are different now. You're much more than simply a necromancer. So, to answer your question bluntly, I would still love the opportunity to meet my grandson, should that be the course things take."

My heart skips a beat and I stop walking. Tears spring to my eyes and I look over my shoulder at him. "It was a boy?"

The corners of his lips curve upward.

I press my fingertips to my lips, trying to keep them from quivering. How do I find my way back there when I don't even know where Wade is?

"I really do admire you, Autumn. There has always been something very special about you. Even when you were facing death as a young child, you did so with a dignity I've rarely seen," he says. "It would be an honor to call you family."

"Then help me find Wade," I say, pleading with him.

He shakes his head, patting my hand and letting go of my arm. "Don't you think I've messed with fate enough?"

Before I have the chance to say anything else, he reaches out, placing a hand on my shoulder. As he steps back from me, I realize we walked in a circle through the cemetery, and we're right back where we started.

"My time is up. I really must go," he says, taking a few more steps backward as the black smoke opens up behind him.

"But—" I begin.

Before I can say another word, he steps into his portal and is gone.

I blow out a puff of defeated air and turn back to Charlotte's grave. "Charlotte, what do you think I should do? Should I hunt down the realty company next? What happens if it's another dead end?"

Kneeling down, I run my hands over my face.

"You look like you could use a friend," a voice says from behind me.

My heart skips a beat as I register the words—the same words that sparked something beautiful a lifetime ago.

No... *it can't be*... Can it?

CHAPTER 28
SECOND CHANCES

My heart practically jumps out of my chest as I scramble around in the snow to face the other direction.

"Angel?" I blurt out.

Wade stands back a few feet, wearing his signature black leather jacket, which disrupts the sea of white all around him in the most beautiful way. My breath catches in my throat and I gape at him.

He really *is* an angel.

His eyes are wide and his mouth hangs slightly agape. Tentatively, he steps forward. "Do I know you?"

I shake my head, trying to calm my heart and mind. I want to tell him everything and rush to get back to the way things used to be, but I know better. Things have to unfold the way they're meant to.

"No...you just startled me," I say, backpedaling.

His silver eyes become narrow slits. "And you make a habit out of calling out for an angel in your moment of need?"

I wince. "I...guess so?" It sounds like more of a question than a statement, and I hope like hell he doesn't think I'm totally insane.

"That's kinda weird," he says, his eyes flashing with that hint of curiosity I know so well and instantly I know what to say next.

"I've been, um...*studying* angels," I say, trying to sound more reasonable. "I'm a student at Windhaven Academy."

A smile erupts across his handsome face. "Really? That's cool. So am I, actually—or I will be next week." He takes another step closer. "Well, I didn't mean to freak you out. I just wasn't expecting to find anyone else out here."

"It's okay," I say, unable to wash away the relief and excitement budding inside me. All I want in the world is to rush over to him and wrap my arms around him and tell him I'll never let him go.

Instead, it's torture staying put and waiting to see if he comes closer.

As I hoped he would, he walks forward, then takes a seat in the snow beside Charlotte's grave. His eyes float across the stone, appraising it.

"She seems nice," he says, smirking.

"Oh, definitely. Great talker, too," I laugh.

He shrugs nonchalantly. "Sure, if you like those Chatty Cathy types."

I burst out laughing. Unable to help myself, I sit down beside him, keeping my knees as close to him as I dare.

"So, what's your name, anyway?" he asks, tipping his chin toward me.

I chew on my lip for a moment, trying to remember why this moment feels so significant. Then, it comes to me.

"Drusilla," I say, the corner of my lips curving upward.

He snorts. "Sure, and my name is *actually* Angel."

My eyes widen, but again I chuckle. "I could totally see that, actually. As long as it's not Angelus, I think we're five by five."

"Ha—quoting Faith, huh? See, now I know you're talking crap," he says, winking at me.

My breath catches and I find myself a puddle right beside him. God, I've missed that wink.

"I knew I'd like you," he says, interrupting my internal gushing.

My eyes widen. "You did?"

"Yeah, I mean, it's not often you find anyone else alive in a graveyard, let alone a beautiful woman with a sense of humor," he says, shooting me a lopsided grin.

My heart melts and I have to work to keep my utter giddiness in check.

"Was that too cheesy?" His face scrunches. "It was, wasn't it?"

I shake my head. "Just enough cheese, I think."

He beams back.

A moment of silence spreads out between us and he clasps his hands between his legs.

"So, is she family?" he asks, pointing to Charlotte's grave.

I shake my head. "No. I don't think I have any family here. I was just in town, so I thought I'd stop and check out the older part of the cemetery. What about you?"

"I came to visit my grandpa. He's over there in the columbarium. But no family over here, as far as I'm aware of."

"So, what brought you to this part of the cemetery,

then?" I ask. I have my own hunches, and I'm sure a certain angel actually did have something to do with it.

"I guess you could say I feel sorta drawn to the spirits here," he says, laughing to himself.

I glance down, trying to hide the smile that springs to my face. If he knew I was actually in on his little joke, I wonder what he'd think? Would it be a relief? Or would it freak him out?

"So, Drusilla, do *you* believe in ghosts?" he asks, flitting his gaze around the headstones.

Taking a moment to think, I'm struck by the déjà vu in the flow of our conversation. There are so many synchronicities, even within the tiny differences from the last time we met.

"Yeah, actually, I do," I say, kicking out my legs and leaning back on my hands.

"Me, too," he says, clearly happy about this statement. "Guess that must be why we both love us a good Buffy reference. We're on the same wavelength."

"Guess so," I agree with a nod. "Well, to be fair, my mom used to make me watch it with her. But who's counting?"

He tips his head back and laughs. "Ah yes, the obligatory Mom duty. I totally get that."

My head snaps up and I quirk an eyebrow. "You do?"

He snickers, making a face. "Well, of course I do. I *do* have a mom, you know. It's not like I was forged or something, as cool as that would be."

I shake my head, trying to knock loose my surprise. "Yeah, of course."

"Anyone ever tell you you're a little odd?" he says, scrunching his face.

Nodding, I say, "On occasion, yes."

"Well, I suppose I better head back," Wade says, standing back up.

"So soon?" I say, pulling my legs in to stand as well.

He reaches a hand out to me, and I accept his offering. Even through my glove, my hand vibrates at his contact and as I rise, the warmth of his body radiates straight through me. My breath hitches as I stand only a few inches from him.

"Thanks," I mutter, releasing his hand and taking a deliberate step back to clear my head.

He blinks, as if he was suddenly under the same spell I was. Inhaling deeply, he releases the breath and nods to himself. "Yeah, my mom's over there paying her respects, but I'm sure she'll be ready to leave soon. She's not dressed for the cold."

I look over his shoulder, beyond him and the gate into the other area of the graveyard. A woman with long brown hair is sitting on the bench just outside the columbarium. Her hand is clutched at her neck as she pulls her winter coat in tighter.

Part of me would love nothing more than to go with him and meet her, but at the same time, I'm terrified.

"Oh, I see. Well, I need to get back to Windhaven, anyway," I say, checking my watch.

"All right. Guess I'll be going, then," Wade says, shifting through the snow. He moves away from me slowly, as if he's fighting the same urge to stay together.

"Okay," I say, biting my lip.

He flashes me another grin and turns on his heel, making his way to the gate. When he reaches it, he turns around, "See ya around, Dru." He winks, opening the gate and walking out.

Everything inside my chest screams to follow him. To kiss him, to give him my number—anything. But somewhere in the back of my mind, I know this is the way it begins.

The hunt. The mystery of it.

We'll both be at Windhaven Academy soon and if he's anything like the Wade from before, he won't stop until he finds out who I really am.

I don't move from my spot in the snow until he and his mom get into a red SUV and drive off. There are so many fighting emotions within me as I make my way to my own vehicle. I'm so happy for Wade. His mother's with him and he still has his father—sort of.

After the way this trip started, I actually feel like everything is really going to be okay.

When I clear the gate, I notice a woman standing beside my vehicle. Her dark hood obscures some of her face, but instantly, I know who she is.

No, no, no...

Everything inside me is screaming to run the other direction—to walk away from this fight. But instead, my feet continue carrying me forward.

"What are you doing here?" I demand. With my fists clenched at my sides, I take a deep breath.

I will not let her take my second chance away.

The woman pushes back her hood, her worn face somehow years lighter now. In her hands are the large shears used to cut the threads of life. The same shears that had stabbed her sister and ended countless lives.

"Aisa," I breathe, narrowing my gaze. Despite myself, my heartbeat quickens.

She grins at me, then slowly places the shears in a holster at her side. "Don't worry, it will be a long while before these shears come for you again."

"How can you be here? I thought I stopped you?" I breathe, fighting back my surprise and terror.

Stepping forward, she reaches out, placing a hand on my shoulder. "Oh, but you did, sweetheart."

"Then... how are you here?" I ask, blinking hard.

"We are inevitable. Should the Moirai cease to exist, there would be no balance to the world. People live, but they still must die. It's the natural order of things. However, what you did was ease the suffering brought to humanity," she says. "You should be very proud of what you accomplished. I wasn't so sure you had it in you." Smirking slightly, she pats my shoulder.

I shake my head. "I don't know what to say."

"You don't have to say anything. Just enjoy your life, Autumn. Make it a good one," Aisa says, her voice far gentler than I remember. "Like your mother, you will have a long while until the end of your thread comes due."

My forehead creases, and I take a step back from her.

"Are you saying I'm immortal?" I ask, surprised.

She shakes her head. "Sadly, no. However, your deeds have not gone unrewarded. Now that things have been... righted, I guess you could say you have inherited longevity from your mother. Something you should always have had. It will be a very long time before death catches up to you."

"Oh," I say, my eyelashes fluttering as I fight to process fully what this means.

"But you should know that in time, however long that

is, you will still face the scales to be judged." Her expression again turns dark and she sighs. "The burden you carry now is a heavy one. I should know."

She points inside my car and I bend down to have a look. Sitting on the passenger seat is the small, intricately carved wooden box.

"Regardless, I'd like to think things played out the way they were meant to," she says with a lopsided sort of grin. "Maybe you could even call it fate."

The End

ALSO BY CARISSA ANDREWS

THE PENDOMUS CHRONICLES

Trajectory: *A Pendomus Chronicles Prequel*

Pendomus: *Book 1 of the Pendomus Chronicles*

Polarities: *Book 2 of the Pendomus Chronicles*

Revolutions: *Book 3 of the Pendomus Chronicles*

DIANA HAWTHORNE SUPERNATURAL MYSTERIES

Oracle: *Book 1*

Amends: *Book 2 (February 26, 2021)*

Immortals: *Book 3 (May 28, 2021)*

Vestige: *Book 4*

Harbinger: *Book 5*

Pantheon: *Book 6*

THE 8TH DIMENSION NOVELS

The Final Five: *An* **Oracle** *&* **Awakening** *Bridge Novelette*

Awakening: *Rise as the Fall Unfolds*

Love is a Merciless God

ABOUT THE AUTHOR

Carissa Andrews
Sci-fi/Fantasy is my pen of choice.

 Carissa Andrews is an international bestselling indie author from central Minnesota who writes a combination of science fiction, fantasy, and dystopia. Her plans for 2021 include continuation of her Diana Hawthorne Supernatural Mysteries. As a publishing powerhouse, she keeps sane by chilling with her husband, five kids, and their two insane husky pups, Aztec and Pharaoh.

To find out what Carissa's up to, head over to her website and sign up for her newsletter:

www.carissaandrews.com

facebook.com/authorcarissaandrews

twitter.com/CarissaAndrews

instagram.com/carissa_andrews_mn

amazon.com/author/carissaandrews

bookbub.com/authors/carissa-andrews

goodreads.com/Carissa_Andrews

Printed in Great Britain
by Amazon